# MILDRED'S
# BOYS AND
# GIRLS

# *The Original Mildred Classics*

# MILDRED'S
# BOYS AND
# GIRLS

*Book Six of*
*The Original Mildred Classics*

## MARTHA FINLEY

CUMBERLAND HOUSE
NASHVILLE, TENNESSEE

MILDRED'S BOYS AND GIRLS
by Martha Finley

Any unique characteristics of this edition:
Copyright © 2001 by Cumberland House Publishing, Inc.

Published by Cumberland House Publishing, Inc.,
431 Harding Industrial Drive, Nashville, Tennessee 37211

Cover design by Bruce Gore, Gore Studios, Inc.
Photography by Dean Dixon Photography
Hair and Makeup by Calene Rader
Text design by Julie Pitkin

ISBN 1-58182-232-4

Printed in the United States of America
1 2 3 4 5 6 7 8 — 05 04 03 02 01

# MILDRED'S

# BOYS AND

# GIRLS

# CHAPTER I

DR. LANDRETH WAS just finishing hasty morning preparations when the room door opened softly, and a sweet child voice said, "Good morning, papa! Breakfus' is ready."

"Ah, good morning, papa's dear pet!" he returned, stooping to kiss the rosebud mouth, whose owner had entered and come close to his side. "Did you get the breakfast?"

"I helped," she answered, drawing up her tiny form with an air of pride and importance. "I set the table for mamma."

"That was right, my little Marcia. Always do all you can to help your good, kind mother," he responded, taking her hand and leading her down to the dining room—a bright, cheery apartment, tastefully and appropriately furnished, faultlessly neat, with June roses peeping in at an east window, whence one caught a glimpse of the river sparkling in the morning sunlight. In the center was a table covered with snowy damask, glittering with silver and china, adorned with sweet-scented flowers fresh from the garden, and well laden with appetizing viands prepared by Mildred's own skillful hands.

"Good morning, my dear," she said, smiling affectionately up into her husband's face as she came in from the kitchen with the steaming coffeepot, Percy following with a plate of hot biscuits. "I hope your sleep has rested and refreshed you."

"Thank you. Yes, wife, but I am ashamed of my self-indulgence when I perceive how much you have accomplished while I have lain like a sluggard in my bed," he returned, bestowing a fond, admiring glance upon her as he helped the little ones into their seats at the table and then took his own.

"Indeed, you need not," she said warmly. "You who were up half the night while your wife and children rested and slept."

"Poor papa! Mama told us 'bout it," put in little Marcia. "She said we mustn't make a noise to wake you till breakfus' was ready."

"Always thoughtful for my comfort," he remarked with an appreciative glance into the sweet face at the opposite end of the table.

"I can echo your words in all truth and sincerity," she responded, returning his glance with one that said even more than her words.

"Milly, my dear," he said with concern, "it is quite too bad that you should be without a servant. I shall do my best today to find one. I did not marry you to make you a kitchen drudge."

"No, and you haven't," she answered, laughing. "It was no fault of yours that my good Gretchen would bestow herself upon Hans just as I had got her well trained in my ways."

"And we cannot consistently blame them for following the example set by ourselves," he said with a humorous look.

"But it is quite too hard on you to have no help."

"Ah, but I am not reduced to that extremity yet!" she returned with a motherly, smiling glance at their eldest son and daughter. "Percy is a great help, and even our little Marcia saves her mother many a step."

"We like to," cried the boy heartily.

"'Deed we do," chimed in his little sister.

"Good children," said their father. "You will never be sorry for having been kind and helpful to your mother, who has always been so kind and good to you."

Half an hour later, the doctor, looking in at the door of the dining room where Mildred was clearing the table with Percy's assistance, said, "I am going out to the country, my dear. Suppose I take Stuart with me, by way of relieving you of a portion of your cares and labors. He, I think, is the rogue who is most apt to get into mischief."

"Oh, yes! Me wants to go wis papa," cried the little four-year-old in delight. "Mamma, det me hat, p'ease."

"Me too, papa?" asked Marcia.

"Can mother spare you?" he said. "I thought you were to be her little helper today."

A shade of disappointment passed over the child's face. Then her brow cleared as she answered, "Oh, yes! I forgot. I'd rather stay this time."

"That's right," he said with an approving look and smile. "You are papa's dear little girl and some other day when mamma does not need you, you shall go with me for a nice long drive."

"Now me's ready, papa," cried Stuart as his mother put his hat on his head and gave him a goodbye kiss.

Mildred followed her husband to the door, as was her wont.

"Don't work too hard, Milly, my dear," he said, bidding her an affectionate goodbye. "Treat me to a cold dinner for once. I can stand that far better than having you worn out with cooking. And don't do the usual amount of sweeping and dusting."

"Trust me not to hurt myself, Charlie," she returned, laughing. "And please don't deny me the pleasure of having an orderly house, and proving my skill as a cook, though I think it's quite all for your sake, for I like dainty dishes myself."

He smiled knowingly, gave her a parting caress, and as he turned to go, said, "I shall be on the lookout for a girl. Perhaps I may be so fortunate as to find one while doing my rounds."

"I thank you. But please to remember that she must be a pretty good one, or I shall consider her worse than none," she answered in a sprightly tone.

Then, turning back into the house, she said, "Come, children, let us make hay while the sun shines and see what a nice neat house and good dinner we can have ready for papa when he comes home."

"Oh, yes!" they cried, Percy adding, "I'll carry out the dishes," and Marcia asking, "Mayn't I sweep the kitchen, mother?"

"No, dear, your little arms are hardly strong enough for that," her mother answered. "But if you will amuse Baby Fan, it will help me very much. You may take her out on the porch where it is nice and shady."

"Percy, you may help me clear the table and wash the dishes.

"What should I do without my dear little boy and girl to help me?" she added, smiling affectionately upon them.

The young faces reflected the brightness of her own, and the children went about their tasks with cheerful alacrity.

Percy's was nearly completed when a slight sound caused both his mother and himself to turn their heads in the direction of the outer door.

There stood a neatly though poorly dressed Negro woman of middle age, holding a little boy by the hand.

"I'se lookin' for a place to wuk, mistis," she said, dropping a curtsy.

"Are you?" said Mildred. "Come in and sit down and tell me what you can do."

"I'se mos'ly used to cookin', mistis, but I kin wash and iron and clean, ef dat's de wuk dat wants doin'," she answered, dropping the child's hand and moving a little farther into the room.

"What is your name and where are you from?" asked Mildred.

A troubled look came over the woman's face, her eyes sought the floor, and there was a moment's hesitation before the answer came. "Dey calls me Rachel, mistis, an' me an' my ole man an' de chil'n libs a little ways—'bout a mile, I reckon—out de town, ober yonder," she said, pointing with her finger. "We's got po' clo'es an' bery little to eat, but all we wants is wuk."

"It would be hard if you couldn't get that," Mildred said in a kindly tone. "You look very nice and neat," she added, giving her a scrutinizing glance. "I will try you, and if I find you a good worker, will gladly give you employment.

11

"You may take off your sunbonnet and begin at once, if you like. I want this kitchen swept and dusted and these vegetables prepared for dinner.

"The little boy can go out and play in the garden, if he can be trusted not to do any mischief."

Rachel's bonnet was already doffed, and a glad look shone in her eyes. "He won't touch nuffin, mistis," she said. "Ef he does, I'se break ebery bone in his body."

"No, no, don't say that," Mildred said reprovingly, "because you don't mean it, and it would be very cruel and wicked if you did.

"He looks like a good boy," she added, giving the child a couple of biscuits and a kindly smile that called up an answering one on the weary little face while his eyes brightened with surprise and delight, for he had had no breakfast that morning and was very hungry.

He began instantly to devour the food with the greatest voracity.

"You, Jim, ain't you got no manners?" inquired his mother, administering a sound slap on the side of his head. "T'ank de lady, and git out de do' fo' yo' begin eatin'. She don' want no crumbs on de flo'."

The child bobbed his head and muttered a word or two with his mouth full, then darted out of the door and disappeared around the corner of the house.

"You must be hungry, too, I think," Mildred said to the mother, then proceeded to give her a meal before setting her to work.

Having swallowed the last morsel of the biscuit, Jim, thrusting his hands into the pockets of his faded and patched trousers, sauntered slowly about the garden, admiring the flowers and fruits but touching nothing.

Presently he came round to the side of the porch where Marcia was building block houses for her own amusement and that of her baby sister.

At the sight of him, she dropped the block she had in her hand, giving a startled "Oh!" that was half surprise and half alarm, in response to which a broad, good-humored grin overspread Jim's face.

"Who are you?" asked Marcia, a little tremulously.

There were very few Negroes in that region of country at that time, and this was her first sight of one.

"I'se Jim," he answered, drawing a step or two nearer and gazing with curiosity and interest at the nearly completed block house.

"Jim what?" she queried.

"Nuffin' but Jim. I comed hyar wid mammy."

"Mammy?" she repeated interrogatively.

"Ya-as," he drawled, with his eyes still fixed on the blocks. "Wha' dat yo' makin'?"

"A house."

"'Spect it fall down fo' long?"

"Yes. That's what is I made it for." And with the word and a blow of baby Fan's hand, the walls tottered and fell.

Jim sprang forward, eager to assist in gathering up the scattered blocks.

"Don't, little boy. Your hands are too black and dirty," Marcia said in a tone of disgust. "Why don't you wash them?"

"Sho' now, missy, dem's clean han's! Mammy wash dem fo' she brunged me hyar," he said, holding them out before his face and gazing searchingly at them.

13

"No," said Marcia, shaking her wise little head. "They're just as black. See?" she said, placing her own little white one alongside his. "Mine don't look that way. Wouldn't you like yours to look clean and nice too?"

"Ya-as, co'se I would. But—but dat brack won't come off."

"Let's try. Mamma always tells 'em, 'Try, try again.' We've got ever such good soap. I'll run up to mamma's room and get it, and some water and a towel." And with the words, she darted into the house, leaving baby Fan gazing at the stranger and putting up her lip ready to cry.

Curiosity was stronger than fear, however, and the threatened wail burst from the baby's lips only as Marcia reappeared upon the scene, half out of breath with her exertions and the weight of the washbowl she carried.

She set it down hastily, to soothe and comfort Fan.

"There, there, baby, don't cry. Sister's here and won't let anything hurt you," she said, putting her arms round the little one and caressing her hair and cheek.

"Now, Jim," she said, turning to their young visitor, "make haste and wash the black off your hands—and your face too, for it's just as dirty."

Getting down on his knees beside the bowl, Jim obediently dipped his hands in the water and began to scrub them vigorously.

Pausing presently and glancing ruefully at them, he said, "'Twon't come off, missy. Didn't I tole yo' so?"

"But you didn't take soap to them," said Marcia. "Take plenty of soap, rub it on hard, and then you'll see."

Jim followed directions to the best of his ability while Marcia looked on, deeply interested in the success of the experiment.

"Hello! What's all this? What are you about here?" cried a boyish voice. And, turning her head, Marcia saw her brother Percy standing in the doorway.

"I'm having that little boy wash the black off his hands," she answered with gravity. "They're very dirty, and he wants to play with us."

"No, no, that's quite a mistake of yours, sis," returned Percy, laughing merrily. "It's their natural color, and it won't come off if he should wash them all day."

"Won't it?" she asked with concern.

"No, certainly not! Mar, you shouldn't have brought these things from mamma's room without her permission.

"But I'll take them back," he added, lifting the bowl and soap from the floor and carrying them away.

Jim shook the water from his hands, then rubbed them dry against his pants, Marcia regarding the proceeding with a look of doubtful approval.

"I'm sorry the black won't come off," she said, "but you can play with us, 'cause if it won't wash off, it won't dirty the blocks."

Meanwhile, Jim's mother was giving satisfaction in the kitchen, showing familiarity with such employment and, at the same time, a willingness to follow directions that was very pleasing to her new mistress.

Dr. Landreth, coming home filled with disappointment because of an entire failure to find a helper for his wife, was most agreeably surprised by her greeting.

"Oh, Charlie, though of course it is quite too soon to make sure, I do think I have found a treasure of a helper! Or, rather, she has found me." And she went on to tell of Rachel's application for work and the satisfaction she had thus far given in the doing of it.

"I am delighted, Milly," he said. "It was certainly a good Providence that sent her, for I have failed in every effort to find a servant of any sort for you, and I cannot bear to see you toiling through the work yourself. I must confess, too, that I have a partiality for the Negro race in that capacity, probably because of early associations."

# CHAPTER II

"DINNER IS ON the table, my dear," Mildred said, leading the way to the dining room, husband and children following. As Dr. Landreth came in at one door, Rachel, bearing a pitcher of water, entered by another. Their eyes met. A sudden paleness overspread the face of the woman, and in her agitation she nearly let the pitcher fall from her hand.

But not seeming to notice her emotion, the doctor merely gave her a word of kindly greeting as he seated himself at the table, then turned his attention to the children.

He scarcely glanced at her as she went and came during the meal but, at its conclusion, stepped into the kitchen.

"Rachel," he said kindly, "you have nothing to fear of me."

"You knows me den, Marse Charlie?" she answered in tremulous tones. "I know'd you, say, de minit I sot eyes on yo'. An', oh, but I'se 'feared yo' 'form on me, an'—an'—I'se boun' to cut my throat, 'fore I'se gwine be dragged back dar."

"I'd be the last person to inform on you, Rachel," he said, "and I hope you will be safe here. I'd like to have you stay, but I ought to tell you, you are not entirely out of danger this side of Canada."

"We's come a long way—Sam an' me, Marse Charlie—wid de chil'n, too, an' we's all wored out an' cayant go no furder till we gets rested," she returned with a sigh that was half a sob. "So, I t'inks we bettah stay an' work fo' you an' yo' wife an' chil'ns, an' if we hears dey's on our track, den we's boun' to run fo' our lives de bes' we kin. Ef you knows, Marse Charlie, ef you eber hears dey's comin'—" she went on, trembling like a leaf.

"I'll certainly give you warning, Rachel, you may depend upon that," he said emphatically, without waiting for the conclusion of her sentence.

The door into the dining room had just opened, and Mildred, standing on the threshold, looking inquiringly from one to the other, her husband gazing with deep sympathy at Rachel as he stood confronting her, she grasping the back of a chair for support while she looked up imploringly into his face, the big tears streaming down her own.

"You may look upon us as friends who will do all in their power to protect and help you, my poor woman," he went on soothingly.

Then, turning to his wife, he added, "Milly, my love, Rachel and I knew each other in the South many years ago. She was, in fact, born on my uncle's plantation. You can guess the rest."

"Yes," cried Mildred, her eyes kindling, "and Rachel, you may be sure you are as safe here as being with friends can make you."

"I t'anks yo' bery kin'ly, mistis, an' I'se do my bery bes' wid de wuk. And I'se sho' yo' an' Marse Charlie ain't gwine to tell nobody whar we's lib befo' we comed hyar?"

"No, we will keep your secret to the best of our ability," the doctor said as he and Mildred left the room together.

"What about the Fugitive Slave Law, Charlie?" Mildred said inquiringly and half under her breath.

"Would you have me keep it, Milly, my love?" he asked, putting an arm around her waist and drawing her to him.

"Never!" she cried, lifting her flashing, fearless eyes to his face. "No earthly power shall ever force me to refrain from assisting any poor, hunted creature to gain freedom from oppression."

"My brave girl!" he responded with a proud, fond smile. "But I am thankful that even that law requires nothing of us till a claim is made."

"Charlie," she cried, "you feel as I do about it! You would never deliver them up to their oppressors?"

"Surely no, love. I will obey the law of the land in everything in which it does not conflict with the higher law of God, but when that is the case, I cannot hesitate to choose to obey God rather than men."

"And He bids us relieve the oppressed, loose the bands of wickedness, undo the heavy burdens, let the oppressed go free, and break every yoke."

"No ambiguity about those commands," he said. "They are so clear and plain that he that runneth may read.

"I have no abuse to heap upon slaveholders, as a class. Many of them are good, God-fearing men who surely think, as I once did myself, that there is no wrong done the Negro by holding him in bondage, provided he is well treated.

"And many of the race seem quite content with their condition, nor should I ever think of inciting one to run away.

"At the same time, I could not have the heart to help in forcibly returning one who had fled and felt that it would be terrible to him to go back. No more would I return a white bound boy or girl fleeing from the oppression of an unkind master or mistress."

"Nor I," said Mildred. "Do you know anything of the man, Rachel's husband, or the treatment they have received?"

"I have not heard their story yet," replied the doctor. "Sam was a likely Negro when I knew him, and that makes me the more afraid there will be a pursuit. But we will not borrow trouble or encourage them to do so.

"We need a man about the place, Milly, to care for my horses, the garden, etc. It may be a good thing, for both them and ourselves, if we employ him also."

Mildred expressed her approval.

"Well, my dear," said the doctor, "if you think best, you may have a talk with Rachel and tell her to bring Sam with her tomorrow morning, early, that I may see and talk with him before beginning my rounds.

"I must go now, for I have several calls to make."

"And Baby Fan is calling her mother," Mildred said, going with him as far as the porch, where the four children were all at play together.

In the course of the afternoon, Mildred seized a favorable opportunity, when alone with Rachel, to draw from her the story of her flight and its cause.

"Mistis," Rachel said, "I wasn't neber 'bused like

some po' blacks. I'se allus had 'nuff cawnbread an'
bacon an' cabbage an' taters an' sich, clo'es to
weah, too; an', w'en I got sick, I wuz tuk care of.
But, mistis, my chil'n wuz sole 'way from me — two
of um dat wuz ol'er dan Jim, — an' Marse George
White, whut owned my Sam (dat's my ole man), he
tuk sick an' died, an' Sam wuz gwine be sole.

"Mistis, I 'specks you knows, dat kas I b'longed to
Marse Cass dat owned de nex' plantation w'en Sam
wuz sole, he wuz boun' to be tuk 'way, w'ile I'd be
lef' behind. We couldn't stan' dat, so we slips out in
de dark night, wi' little Jim an' de baby — de two
chil'n we hab lef' — an' trable, trable to'ds de norf
star, fas' as eber we could, hidin' in de daytimes,
an' trablin' nights, till we gits 'mos' to dis place.

"Den we's so beat out, — feets soah an' bleedin',
mis'ry in de back, mis'ry all ober — we couldn't go
no furder, so we jes drap down by de roadside,
'hind de bushes, an' lay dar long time.

"We ain't got nuffin to eat, an' we's pow'ful hungry. We doan' want to steal, but Sam, he's 'bliged
to go git a few eahs of green cawn out'n a field,
kase we wuz starvin'.

"He's gwine in de night, an' dere doan' nobody
see him, an' de nex' mawnin' we's trable on agin fo'
de sun up.

She went on to tell of their joy at finding a little
deserted log cabin, half in ruins, deep in the thick
woods, and how they established themselves there,
making a bed of the dry leaves the wind had
whirled into one corner and subsisting on such
small game as they could trap, fish caught in a
neighboring stream, and roots and berries, and
eked out by Sam's small earnings from odd jobs
done for farmers in the vicinity.

Mildred listened to the story with tears in her eyes.

"And is that miserable cabin the only home you have?" she asked as Rachel paused in her narrative.

"Yes, mistis, but 'tain't so bad while de wedder's warm an' de sun shines. An' Sam, he 'lows he'll fix hit up fo' winter.

"Dar's lots ob dry sticks on de groun' in de woods to make fiahs wid, an' ef we gits wuk, we kin buy wahm clo'es to weah an' plenty to eat," she added hopefully. "Oh, mistis, we's do well nuff ef de slave catchers doan' fin' us!" she concluded with a paling cheek and a hurried glance toward the outer door.

Mildred's heart was wrung with pity. She said what she could to reassure and comfort the poor hunted creature, bidding her put her trust in God and reminding her that, even should she be carried back to bondage, in another and better world she would be free and never again called to part from those she loved.

"Dat's so, mistis," Rachel said, wiping her eyes. "An' de deah good Lawd knows hit's all de comfort we uns hab in dis worl'"

"I trust better times are dawning for you, Rachel," Mildred responded. "I shall do what I can to make you comfortable here, and my husband thinks he can give Sam employment, too, in taking care of the horses, the cow, and the garden."

"Oh, mistis! Dat's be bery wuk Sam kin do de bes'." Rachel cried, a gleam of joy lighting up her sad face for a moment.

"Ah, there is the doctor now!" exclaimed Mildred, glancing from the window. "And is that Sam with him, Rachel?"

"Yes, mistis, dat my ole man, sho' nuff! An' dey's gwine to de garden, ain't dey?" Rachel said eagerly, hopefully, her eyes following the direction of Mildred's gaze.

"Yes, my husband must have engaged him, at least on trial."

"T'ank de Lawd! Now we's bofe got wuk, an' de chil'n woan' hab to go hungry no mo'!" exclaimed Rachel with a sigh of relief.

Dr. Landreth came in presently, looking even more bright and cheery than was his wont. "Well, my dear," he said in a tone of satisfaction, "I have found and engaged Sam. I have also bought a little one-story frame building, which is to be moved tomorrow onto the lower end of the lot and will, I think, make quite a comfortable dwelling for him and his family."

"Oh, Charlie! How nice!" cried Mildred. "It will be so very convenient to have them close at hand yet not in the house. I shall feel quite like a Southern matron," she added laughingly. "You were fortunate in finding the little frame house all ready to your hand."

"Yes, and so near. It's that one across the street, the one Smith, the butcher, has been occupying. Ormsby has purchased the lot, which adjoins his, you know, with a view to enlarging his grounds. He was glad to part with the building, saying it was only in his way."

Just then Annis Keith, Mildred's youngest sister, came in.

"What a nice-looking black woman I saw in your kitchen door as I passed," she said. "Where in the world did you find her, Milly, and is she going to stay?"

Mildred replied, giving the whole story.

"Oh, that's nice!" said Annis. "I heard Wallace say he had bought that lot and wanted to get rid of the house. So Charlie has purchased it?

"I'll tell you what, Milly, we must help you to furnish it for these poor folks. There's an old carpet at home that I know mother will be willing to spare them, a bedstead, too, and probably some few other things."

"Thank you," said Mildred heartily. "I can provide a bed, sheets, quilt, and blanket."

"And anything else that is needed," added the doctor.

"And among all the members of our three families, half-worn clothes enough to dress them all decently can surely be found," supplemented Annis, springing to her feet. "I'll start this minute on a collecting tour and see what I can get out of mother and Zillah."

"It is very good in you to undertake it, but don't tax them too heavily," Mildred said, smiling up at her. "You know both are inclined to give, even beyond their ability.

"Ah! There is mother at the gate now. Yes, and Zillah, too." And she hurried to the door to greet and bring them in.

"Zillah has just been telling me of Wallace's sale to Charlie and about these poor people that have come to you," Mrs. Keith said as she seated herself in the easy chair Mildred drew forward for her. "I suppose they must be very destitute, and so they have come in particularly to talk with you girls about what can be done among us to supply their immediate wants."

"Just like you, mother," remarked the doctor,

giving her an appreciative look and smile. "I trust you ladies will not shut me out from the conference?"

"Oh, no, no, indeed!" they all exclaimed, Mildred adding, "Nor from the privilege of giving as liberally as you please to so worthy an object."

The result of it all—the conference and the united effort—was that, by the end of the week, Sam and Rachel found themselves comfortably established in the snuggest little home they had ever known and were working with steady industry for their kind benefactors. Most of their time was employed in the service of the Landreths but some of it in occasional odd jobs for the Keiths and Ormsbys. But let their toil be for whom it might, it was sure to be well rewarded. Rachel proved very competent as a cook, washer, and ironer; Sam no less so in his own peculiar sphere. Both so conducted themselves as to gain the respect and hearty liking of all with whom they had to do.

The fugitives would have been very happy in their new home could they have banished from their minds the fear of pursuit and an enforced return to bondage. But alas, it was ever present with them, the weary, hunted look seldom absent from their faces. They seemed to shrink from intercourse with the townspeople outside of the three families who employed them, and the presence of a stranger always caused them uneasiness. They would start and tremble at the sound of an approaching footstep or break off in the midst of a laugh or jest to glance apprehensively toward the outer door.

It was as if the sword of Damocles hung continually over their heads.

Yet as time passed on, summer waned into autumn, winter followed, then spring and summer came again and went, and they were still unmolested, a feeling akin to security crept over them. Their faces lost the worn, haggard look, and there was something lighthearted in their words and ways. But alas, security is not safety.

# CHAPTER III

THE HARVEST WAS past. The wheat and corn had all been garnered, fruits and vegetables stored for winter use. The ripe nuts were dropping in the woods, and the trees hung out merry banners of crimson and gold, varied with many shades of red, russet, and green, and had strewn the ground with a carpet of the same brilliant hues. The days were warm and bright; the nights chilly with frost, harbinger of winter, stern and cold.

Rachel dreaded the Northern winter. She had suffered from the cold during the previous one, in spite of an abundance of fuel and warm clothing provided by her liberal-minded employers. Gladly would she have returned to her native place if she could have drawn the breath of freedom there, but bondage was worse by far, in her esteem, than the bitterest cold, And Sam was like-minded with herself.

"De nights am gettin' awful chilly," she remarked one evening as she heaped fuel upon the fire in her stove in the cozy room that served them as kitchen, dining room, and parlor. "Winter's cumin' fas', an' I wisht it was ober."

"Does yo' wan' to be a trablin' to'wds de Souf?" queried Sam with a grin as he hitched his chair up closer to the stove and held out his hands over it to feel the pleasant warmth.

"Co'se I does," she laughed in return.

"Yo's wouldn't git no sich suppah down dar as yo's a-preparin' now," remarked Sam, sniffing up with delight the combined odors of steaming coffee, fresh sausage, potatoes roasting, and cornbread baking in the oven.

"Dat's so!" she responded, setting a jug of molasses and a plate of butter on the table. Then, stepping to the cupboard again, she brought out a plate of ginger cakes and a pie.

"Dar wasn't no starvin' on ole master's plantation, but we uns dat did de wuk didn't hab de luxuries ob life what de w'ite folks is 'joyin' mos'ly ebery time dey sets down to de table," she continued, coming back to the fire to turn her sausage and peep into the oven.

"Dis cookstove ain't, ob co'se, quite ekal to de one in Marse Charlie's kitchen," she remarked as she pushed the oven door to again, "but it's putty good, an' I 'spec's dat cawnbread ain't gwine a-beggin' dis hyar night."

"Is I gwine to hab 'lasses on mine, mammy?" queried Jim, who was seated opposite to his father with a well-thumbed primer in his hand.

"Co'se, chile, didn't I tole you so w'en yo' readed dat putty piece to me? Dat chile's larnin' mighty fas', Sam, yo' bettah b'leeb," she added in an aside to her husband and with a glance of motherly pride directed toward her eldest hope. "Marse Percy's gibin' him lessons 'mos' ebery day, an' I reckon hit's po'w'ful good teachin', 'cuz dat boy Jim, he ain't so awful smart nohow; we knows dat."

The latter part of the sentence was uttered in a higher key, as intended for Jim's benefit.

"'Co'se not, but he's boun' to grow smarter ef he sticks to de book," responded Sam with a chuckle of satisfaction and parental pride.

"I'se gwine ter, daddy," said Jim. "I'se gwine ter learn a hep o' tings fro' Marse Percy. He knows lots, Marse Percy does."

"Co'se he do," said Rachel. "Now you, Jim, set de chars up to de table; suppah's ready."

Jim hastened to obey, and all gathered about the table and partook of the smoking viands with keen appetites and great enjoyment.

Then Rachel cleared the table, washed the dishes, put the children to bed, and sat down to the work of patching an old coat of Sam's while he smoked his pipe and nodded in his chair beside the stove.

Someone knocked, then Percy Landreth, putting his head in at the door, called out in a happy, boyish treble, "Hello, Sam! Father wants you to saddle the gray mare and bring her round to the front gate just as quickly as you can, for he has been sent for to the country in a great hurry. Somebody's very sick, I suppose."

"Yes, sah, Marse Percy. I'll hab her roun' quick as I kin," responded Sam, rising and shaking the ashes from his pipe on the stove hearth.

Laying the pipe on a shelf, he picked up an old hat from the floor and hurried out in the direction of the stables, while Percy, bidding Rachel a kindly good night, bounded away toward home.

A few moments later he reported to his father that the mare was at the gate, waiting.

The doctor had his overcoat on, his hat in his hand, and only taking time for a hasty parting kiss to his wife, who, as was her wont, had followed him to the door, he ran down the path and vaulted into the saddle.

"I may not be back till morning, Sam," he said, "so you needn't wait up for me. If I get home sooner, I'll either rouse you or put the mare into her stall myself."

With the last word, he galloped swiftly away and in a moment was lost to sight in the gathering darkness.

Mildred went in and closed the door, sighing softly to herself as she thought of the night of wakefulness and unrest her husband had in prospect after a day of toil, both mental and physical.

Percy heard the sigh and read her thoughts in her speaking countenance.

"Mother," he said, looking up affectionately and inquiringly into her face, "why does my father lead such a hard life—at everybody's beck and call, often losing his night's rest, and sometimes his meal but half-eaten? Is it just to make a living for us all?"

"No, my son, that is not even his principal object. But he has a noble ambition to be of the greatest possible service to his fellow men and to use every God-given talent to the glory of Him who gave it."

"Mother, I am proud of my father!" cried the boy, and his eyes sparkled and flashed as he spoke. "And yet it makes me sorry to see him working so hard."

Sam was saying the same thing to himself as he slouched homeward, for he was very fond of the doctor, who had proved so kind a friend to him.

"'Clare to goodness," he said as he relighted his pipe and settled himself again beside the fire, "'Clare to goodness ef de doctah doan' had de worstes' time

30

ob enny ob us, gittin' up outen his warm bed on de col'est nights and trablin' wy out in de kentry, time an' agin, to see de sick folks what maybe mout jes' as well a-sent fer him long fo' sundown."

"Dat's so," responded Rachel, "an' many's de time he doan' git home to his dinnah till ebery bressed ting's stone cole, less all dried up, wid us folkses tryin' our bes' to keep 'em warm.

"Is yo' gwine to wait up fo' Marse Charlie, Sam?"

"No, co'se not, w'en dar's no tellin' ef he'll git back fo' mawnin'."

"How'd I know dat?" she queried. "Dar!" she said, breaking off her thread. "Dat ole coat's ready fo' yo' to weah in de mawnin', an' I'se gwine to bed quick as a wink, cuz I'se dat sleepy I cayn't hole me eyes open no longer."

In a few moments the lamp was out, darkness and silence reigned in the little home, and parents and children slept the sound sleep of innocence and peace. "The sleep of the laboring man is sweet," and Rachel and Sam, having toiled from early morning, were now tasting that sweetness to the full.

Time flew by on viewless wings. In one after another of the neighboring houses, and in the more distant ones that composed the town, lights were extinguished, and old and young sought their pillows till, as midnight drew on, scarce a creature was stirring, indoors or out, through the whole length and breadth of the place.

In compliance with her husband's earnest request, Mildred had, at the usual hour, closed the house and gone to bed with her children.

As it was not probable that the doctor could return before morning, and he had taken a night key with which he could admit himself, she soon ceased to listen for his coming and dropped asleep.

There was no moon, but the stars shone in a clear sky, and a slight breeze now and then sent a shower of leaves falling through the chill, frosty air.

At length, an intently listening ear might have heard, far away in the distance, the low rumble of wheels.

It drew nearer, nearer, and more distinct — so near that, had Mildred been awake, she would doubtless have sprung from her couch, thrown up her window, and looked out to see what it meant.

But she slept on, and presently the vehicle — a rough farm wagon without springs — turned into the lane that led past her garden fence to the humble little dwelling that sheltered Sam and Rachel.

It was drawn by two stout horses. A man on the front seat was driving, another sat by his side, and a third pushed on a trifle ahead on horseback.

This last seemed to be the leader. When he had reached the door of the little house that sheltered his intended victims, he halted, drew rein, and spoke in a subdued tone to the others.

"This must be the place. Hist! No noise, for if we can but catch them asleep, we may hope to get away with them without any disturbance. Have your weapons ready for instant use, but remember, there is to be no unnecessary violence.

"Jones, hitch to that fence and give your assistance to Collins and me in the capture, for the more of us there are, the surer and quicker work we can make.

"You both know what's to be done, screams or any sound that might rouse the neighbors to be prevented if possible."

He alighted, fastened his horse, and stepped softly to the door.

It had a strong bolt that resisted his effort to open it.

But Jones, coming up, whipped out a knife and, working vigorously with it for few minutes, succeeded in removing a panel, then put in his hand and drew back the bolt, throwing the door wide open, and the three rushed upon their sleeping, innocent victims.

Both Sam and Rachel were gagged and bound hand and foot before they were fairly awake. A few half-stifled groans were the only sounds they were able to utter as they were dragged from the house and thrown into the wagon.

"Pity we couldn't give 'em time to dress," remarked Collins. "Some danger that they'll catch their death of cold, and that wouldn't pay, would it, Mr. Cass?"

"No, but we'll tumble their duds into the wagon and put the bedclothes on top. That, with the good bed of hay under it, will keep them from freezing."

"The light of a dark lantern was thrown into the room long enough to enable the captors to gather up the sleeping children, clothing, and bedclothes. The little ones—so as not to awaken them to rouse the neighbors with their cries—were laid gently down beside their parents. Blankets and sheets were tucked carefully over and about them all, their clothes tumbled upon top of the heap. The horseman mounted his steed, the others their seat in the wagon, and as quietly as they could, the kidnappers set out on their return, carrying their wretched captives with them.

The whole thing had been done so expeditiously,

and with so little noise or disturbance of any kind, that not a soul in the neighborhood had been aroused. Not a sound but the rumble of the wheels and the thud of the horses' hoofs broke the solemn stillness of the night as they pursued their way through the lane and down the road beyond.

Meanwhile, Dr. Landreth had succeeded in so far relieving his patient that he felt warranted in leaving her for a time, and now he was on his homeward way.

Within a mile of the town he heard, to his surprise, sounds that told of the approach from that direction of a wagon.

"Who," he asked himself, "could be abroad at that hour, and for what purpose? Had sickness or accident sent someone out in search of medical or surgical aid? Mildred knew where he could be found and had perhaps directed them accordingly.

He reined in his horse as they drew near. The outline of objects could be dimly discerned by the starlight.

"Holoow!" he called, "any assistance wanted there?"

"None, thank you," replied the other horseman. "We're all right. I'm merely moving some of my goods and chattels and have all the assistance I need."

"You choose an odd time for it, friend," returned the doctor in a tone of surprise and incredulity, but the other rode on without response, was perhaps already too far away to catch his words.

The doctor wheeled his horse to look after the retreating forms, but they had already vanished in the darkness, and he jogged on again toward home, musing, half sleepily—for he was very weary from his day's work and the vigil of the night — on a strangely familiar tone in the voice that had just replied to his query.

It seemed to him, too, that a faint sound, as of one in distress, had come from the wagon as it passed.

Just as he turned into the lane, on reaching his own premises, a sudden thought flashed upon him, instantly rousing all of his faculties to their fullest extent.

"Is that it?" he exclaimed aloud. "Are they the goods and chattels they're carrying off? Ah! I know now where that voice belongs, and, Joe Cass, I'll rescue your prey from your talons if I can."

He had urged his mare to a rapid trot and in another moment drew rein beside the little frame house where he had established the fugitives from slavery in such comfort.

The door stood wide open, and all was darkness and silence. He dismounted hastily, hurried in, struck a match, and glanced around.

It was a scene of confusion that met his gaze: the table pushed into one corner, chairs overturned, the bed stripped of its covering, stray articles of clothing dropped here and there, and not a living soul within or without.

"They've made a clean sweep," he said, half aloud, "man, woman, and child."

He hurried out, remounted, and proceeded with all haste to arouse one neighbor after another, beginning with his brother-in-law, Wallace Ormsby.

In Pleasant Plains there was, as in most of the towns of the North at that time, a division of sentiment on the subject of slavery. Some favored the institution and insisted that it be let alone where it was and that escaped slaves be returned to their masters, while others were fierce in their denunciations of all slaveholders, indiscriminately, and of the law that required all citizens of the United States, when called upon, to assist masters in reclaiming their escaped slaves.

Dr. Landreth had been long enough a resident of the place to know to whom to make his appeal, and with the first beams of the rising sun, a party of a dozen or more men, well mounted, had started in pursuit.

Ormsby was one of them, but the doctor was detained at the last moment by an urgent call to a man in a fit.

"I'm afraid that, after all, it's but a fool's errand we are on," remarked a man named Foote to Wallace Ormsby as they left the town. "You know the law gives the slaveholder a right to claim a runaway."

"Yes, but we will at least give him some trouble in doing so—bring him back with the fugitives and make him prove property—if only to teach the arrogant knaves that they can't make a raid upon our towns by night and carry off peaceable citizens without let or hindrance."

"It's an iniquitous law and should not be permitted to be enforced," spoke up another horseman in their rear.

"Then let us exert ourselves for its repeal," said Wallace.

"So we will, so we will!" exclaimed a number of voices, "and in the meanwhile do what we can to help these poor creatures to escape."

# CHAPTER IV

THAT WAS A terrible awakening brought to Sam and Rachel by their cruel captors. Roused from profound slumber by the rude thrusting of the gag into their mouths and the binding of their limbs, with what anguish of mind they felt themselves dragged from their warm beds into the frosty outer air and unceremoniously tumbled into the wagon, to lie there shivering and vainly trying to shriek for help for moments that must have seemed like hours!

Well they knew the meaning of it all. That they and their children were about to be carried back into that bondage from which they had fled was worse than death.

It was small consolation that no one of the family was being left behind, that they were all sharers in the misfortune, they were together now. But separation would soon follow their arrival at their journey's end.

They had been taken at a disadvantage, and were utterly helpless, utterly at the mercy of their captors, not being able to so much as raise a cry for help.

Great was their mental anguish. Their terror and despair were beyond words, and added to this was no small amount of physical suffering from the distension of their jaws by the gag, the tightness of the cords that bound their limbs, and the numbing coldness of the night air, for the covers that were hastily thrown over them were soon shaken off by the jolting of the wagon, and they could neither replace them nor ask to have it done for them.

Devoutly they wished the children would wake and scream, but they did not do so till they had reached the depths of a thick wood so far from human habitation that the cry wakened only the echoes and was of no avail.

It was now broad daylight, and presently the leader ordered a halt and, coming to the side of the wagon, spoke to his prisoners.

"I reckon you know me, Sam and Rachel," he said in a not unkindly tone, "and you know that what I say, I'll do. I've taken this long journey, expressly to catch you and carry you back to your old homes, and I mean to do it. I don't want to be unnecessarily cruel, and I'm going to loose you and let you up long enough to put on your clothes and have a bite of breakfast. But I'm bound you shan't escape, and shall shoot you without a moment's hesitation if you attempt it.

"Do you hear?" he asked as Collins, at a sign from him, removed the gag from Sam's mouth.

"Yes, sah," groaned the poor fellow, his eyes rolling with terror. "Oh, Marse Cass, ef yo's got enny compassion, hab mercy an' let us go. I'se wuk my fingers to de bone to buy Rachel an' de chil'n.'

"Come, come, Sam, there's no use in pleading. You've got to go back," Cass answered sternly.

"An' be sole 'way from my wife an' chil'n?" Sam's tones were inquiring and tremulous with emotion.

"You deserve it for running off, you cur," said Jones, untying the last of the cords that bound him.

Collins had relieved Rachel also from the gag and was loosing her bonds.

She struggled to her knees and, with clasped hands and streaming tears, begged for mercy for herself, husband, and children.

"We're not going to hurt you, if you keep quiet and don't try to escape," said Cass.

"But I wants to be free, Marse Cass," she sobbed. "I'se cayn't stan' it to be gwine back to have my ole man sole 'wy from me an' de chil'ns."

"You've got to," was the dogged reply. "And you may think yourself well off that I don't promise you a sound flogging for running away. You'd no cause, for I always treated you well."

"S'pose somebody wuz gwine sole you 'way fum de mistis, Marse Cass, what yo'—"

"Be quiet and put on your clothes," he commanded sternly. "Then dress the children."

A terrified silence had fallen upon the latter, and they submitted without a word as, with trembling hands, their mother essayed to obey the order in regard to them.

Some cold cornbread was now distributed among the captives (their captors had something better), but Rachel was too heartbroken to eat.

Cass observed it with indifference, remarking that she was welcome to fast till hunger should make what was provided acceptable to her.

The halt was not for long. Soon the two older captives were again bound, and the wagon moved on, Cass now following and covering them with his revolver.

He was determined to frustrate the endeavor to

escape, which he thought might probably be made, and being also not without some fear of an attempt at rescue on the part of the people of Pleasant Plains, he listened intently for any sound of pursuit and occasionally ventured to take his eyes from the prisoners for a moment to send a backward glance along the road already passed over, to make sure that no pursuer was in sight.

Jones, noting his uneasiness, at length asked with a coarse laugh, "What'll you do, Mr. Cass, if some o' them abolitionists gits after us? Will ye be for fightin' 'em?"

"Wait till the time comes, and you will see," was the cool, half-contemptuous rejoinder.

"P'raps it won't be long he'll have to wait, sir," remarked Collins, pointing to a cloud of dust a mile or so in their rear.

Cass, too, sent a hasty glance in that direction, then gave the command, "Whip up your horses, boys. They've been going at a snail's pace for the last half hour!"

"It's no use," said Jones, complying with the order nevertheless as he made the protest, "They're worn out. Been on the go almost constant since the middle of yesterday afternoon, and here 'tis nearly noon again."

The sting of the lash goaded them for a moment into a trot, but it was impossible for the jaded animals to keep it up, and they presently subsided into a walk again.

"You see, it's no use, sir," said Jones. "But," he added, nodding toward a thicket just then brought into view by a turn in the road, "p'raps we might hide our load and let 'em think they've made a mistake in s'posin' we've been on a slave raid at all."

"The turn in the road would conceal the movement," said Cass rather doubtfully. And with another backward glance then, as the sound of many horses' hoofs and a confused murmur of voices drew rapidly nearer, he said, "But there isn't time. They're just upon us."

He grasped his revolver more firmly as he spoke.

"Is it a fight, sir? Shall we fire on 'em?" asked Collins and Jones in a breath.

"Not till I give the word." And even as he spoke, a wild shout arose.

"Hurrah! We have them, the kidnappers and man stealers! On to the rescue!" And instantly they were surrounded by the pursuing band of horsemen, who pressed close upon them with scowling looks and muttered threats. "Steady, steady, no violence!" cried Wallace Ormsby, who seemed to be the acknowledged leader.

Cass, Collins, and Jones each held his revolver cocked and ready to fire, and they observed with pleasure that the rescuing party were not nearly so well armed as themselves.

Cass straightened himself in the saddle, and glancing about him with a haughty and defiant air, demanded, "May I ask, sirs, what is the meaning of this hostile demonstration?"

"May I ask, sir," returned Ormsby, "by what right you steal into our town by night, break into one of its houses, and violently carry off its peaceable inhabitants?"

"By the natural right to take my own property wherever I can find it," returned Cass with *hauteur*. "You have heard of the Fugitive Slave Law, I presume?"

As he spoke, a cry of distress came from the

wagon, where Sam and Rachel lay bound and helpless but not gagged. "Oh, save us, Marse Ormsby! Dey's gwine tote us back to de lan' ob bondage!"

There was a restless movement among the would-be rescuers. They pressed closer to the wagon, with a muttered threat or two of punishment to be visited upon the kidnappers from some, a word or two of hope and cheer to the captives from others.

"Yes," replied Wallace, "I am not unacquainted with the provisions of that iniquitous law, but I think sir, you will have to go back and prove property before you will be allowed to carry away these poor creatures against their will."

"There will be no difficulty about that," said Cass. "I have ample proof to show, so it strikes me that you might as well refrain from interference, as you will gain nothing in the end and only cause me serious detention."

"Assertions are easily made," said Ormsby, "and we insist upon all the advantages the law will give us, or rather, these poor, innocent victims of yours."

"Very well, sir," returned Cass, "since you outnumber us four to one, and, though we are better armed, I am averse to bloodshed. I will go back and appeal to the law to sustain me in my efforts to recover my property."

He signed to his men to turn their horses' heads in the opposite direction and placed himself again in the rear of the wagon. Ormsby's men fell into line on each side of it, he himself galloped on a few paces ahead, and so they returned to the town.

Mildred, after sleeping but lightly the greater part of the first half of the previous night, had at length fallen into a slumber so deep and profound that she slept on till the sun rose, hearing nothing whatever of the coming or going of the kidnappers or the return of her husband, who, not caring to disturb her and wishing to start the pursuing party with all possible despatch, did not enter his own house after making the discovery of the abduction until breakfast time.

"How late I am!" was her first thought, and she sprang from the bed and began to quickly ready herself for the day. "And Charlie has not come back! Rachel, too, seems to be late, but perhaps I missed her knock and Percy has let her in. Ah, there is a ring at the front door! Who can be coming so early? Somebody wanting the doctor, I suppose. I hope they'll not keep him from his breakfast when it's ready."

She went to a front window, threw it up, and looked out.

"Zillah! Is anything wrong? Anybody sick?"

"Come down as quickly as you can, and I'll tell you!" her sister replied in such evident excitement and agitation that Mildred's heart beat very fast as she hastily descended the stairs and undid the fastenings of the outer door.

"What is it?" she asked, half breathlessly. "Is mother—"

"No, there's nothing wrong with her! But, Milly, kidnappers were here in the night, and they have carried off Sam and Rachel and their children. The doctor discovered it when he came in from the country, somewhere in the small hours. Indeed, he feels quite sure he passed them on the road, but he never thought, at the moment, who or what they were.

"He found the door of their house standing wide open, nobody there, things scattered about, and chairs, etc., overturned in a way that showed him at once what had happened.

"Then he came to our house and roused Wallace, and from there went on till he gathered up quite a large party to go in pursuit."

"And have they gone?" Mildred asked with a blanching cheek as Zillah paused for breath.

"Yes, they've just started, Wallace acting as leader. Oh, Milly, Milly! I'm terribly anxious lest there should be bloodshed."

"I hope not! I think it will not come to that," Mildred answered a little tremulously. "Is—is Charlie—"

"He didn't go with the rest," interrupted Zillah. "He would have, I think, but old Mr. Atkins was found in a fit, and he had to hurry off there just as the party was about to start, and of course they couldn't wait if they meant to overtake the kidnappers."

"No, certainly not," assented Mildred with a satisfied sigh. "Oh, how sorry I am for those poor creatures. They did so dread just what has happened!"

Marcia had followed her mother down the stairs and stood listening in wide-eyed astonishment.

"What, mother, what?" she asked in wonder and dismay, clinging to Mildred and gazing up into her face in a half-frightened way. "What's kidnappers? Do they bite? Do they eat folks up like lions and tigers?"

"Pooh! they're men, goosie," said Percy, he, too, having hurried down to hear what aunt Zillah had to tell. "But mother, mother, are uncle Wallace and the rest going to shoot them?"

"Oh, no! Surely not, Percy!"

"No," said Zillah. "Wallace said they would be

brought back and made to prove property, or compelled to release their prisoners and go back where they came from empty-handed."

"I want to look at the house. May I, mother?" asked Percy.

"Yes, if you will come back directly," she said.

"Oh!" he cried the next moment, speaking from the outer kitchen door, "there are ever so many people round it, inside, too! I can see them through the windows. Mother and auntie, do just come and look! More are coming, too! I suspect everybody in town has heard about it."

The town was indeed full of excitement, and Mildred found herself so agitated with anxieties and fears for poor Rachel and the others—having become really attached to them in the many months that they had served her—that it was with difficulty she could give her mind to the preparation of breakfast and other household cares and duties devolving upon her as mistress of a family.

The meal was just ready to set on the table when the doctor came hurrying in.

"You have heard, Milly?" he said inquiringly, coming to her side and putting an arm round her waist.

"She nodded assent, her heart too full for speech. Then, dropping her head on his shoulder, she sobbed out, "Oh, my poor, poor Rachel! Must she be carried back and have her husband sold away from her?"

"I fear so," the doctor said in a moved tone. "I very much fear Cass will be able to show that he has the law on his side and that all we can do is to add somewhat to his difficulties in carrying out his plans."

"Poor, poor Rachel!" repeated Mildred in a choking voice.

The children stood looking and listening in wonder and distress.

"What's the matter with her, mamma?" queried little Stuart.

"A cruel man is taking her far away, and we cannot have her with us any more."

"I don't like that! I will have my Rachel!" he said, beginning to cry.

"Father," cried Percy, "isn't it very wicked for them to do so? To steal a man and woman and children, and carry them where they don't want to go?"

"I think it is. I believe, as the Declaration of Independence puts it, that 'all men are created equal; that they are endowed by their Creator with certain inalienable rights; that among these are life, liberty, and the pursuit of happiness.' But there was a time when I thought slavery right, and I don't doubt that these men think so now."

"Oh, I'm afraid those bad men will come some night and steal us too!" exclaimed Marcia, beginning to cry, with little Fan joining in, "I'se 'fraid dey will! I'se 'fraid dey will! Papa, don't go 'way and leave us anymore."

"No, no, dears, there's not the least danger of that," their father hastened to say. "They don't want you."

"Why not, papa? Ain't we as nice as the little black children?" asked Marcia, drying her eyes.

"Much nicer, I think" he said with a smile of amusement. "But they don't want you, because— fortunately for you and all of us—your skin is white. But come, let us sit down to the table. The nice breakfast mamma has prepared is getting cold."

Percy, who was a remarkably bright, intelligent boy, had his attention now drawn to the subject for the first time and deluged his father with questions in regard to slavery in America—its history, the laws in regard to it, etc.

The doctor answered patiently for a while, then said, "My son, I haven't time to tell you more about it now. I have been up all night, and I must finish my breakfast and try to get a little sleep before starting out again to visit patients. I will say to you, as the mother of Sir William Jones used to say to him, 'Read, and you will know.' It shall be my business to provide you with the needed books in due time.

"In the meanwhile," he concluded with a smiling glance at his wife, "your mother, I am sure, is quite able to answer any or all of your questions, if she thinks it best to do so."

Little Marcia spoke up suddenly, as if struck with a new idea. "Oh, I just wish I'd got that black washed off Jim's face and hands! 'Cause then the bad men wouldn't have stolen him."

"Did you try?" asked her father.

"Yes, indeed, papa, two or three times. The first time I got water and soap and told him to wash himself. Afterwards I tried, but it wouldn't any of it come off."

"No, my child, because the coloring matter lies deeper than the skin." With the last word, the doctor pushed back his chair, rose, and saying, "I am going up to our room now, wife, to try to get a nap, but don't hesitate to call me if a messenger should come from either of my very sick patients," he left the room.

"Percy, dear," Mildred said, glancing at the clock, "breakfast is unusually late this morning and you and Marcia will barely reach school in time if you start at once."

"Oh, mother," they cried in chorus, "we couldn't study today, and you have no girl, so mayn't we stay and help you?"

"Yes," she replied after a moment's thought. "I doubt if you could attend to lessons, for I feel that it will be difficult for me to think of anything but our poor friends until their fate is decided."

The whole town was in a ferment of excitement over the events of the past night, and hot discussions of slavery and the Fugitive Slave Law were the order of the day in the streets, the stores, the offices, and even the dwellings, for some families were divided in opinion as to the relative rights of slaveholders, non-slaveholders, and of those held in bondage.

The return of the pursuing party was looked for with deep interest, especially by the three families in whose employ the fugitives had been since coming to the place.

Annis Keith came to her sister's help, hurrying in directly after breakfast, full of condolences and lamentations over the misfortune to Sam and his family.

"I had grown really attached to Rachel," she remarked. "She was a most faithful creature, and I wish with all my heart the man may fail to prove ownership."

"I fear there is very little hope of that," Mildred returned sadly. "And my heart aches for the poor woman—to say nothing of Sam and the children! Just think if I were in danger of having my husband sold away from me! To lose him so would surely break my heart."

48

# CHAPTER V

FOR MILDRED, THE day wore slowly away, very slowly, though she had a good deal to do as wife, mother, and housekeeper, was destitute of servants, and received more calls than usual from friends and acquaintances, all desirous to hear whatever she might have to tell of the event which was for the moment the subject uppermost in almost every mind.

But at last it had come to an end. Supper was over, everything cleared away, and the children were in bed, except Percy, who sat by her side studying his lessons for the next day. The doctor was out among his patients, and she—full of anxious, exciting thought—was forcing herself to sit quietly sewing by the light of the lamp on the center table while striving to cast all care for herself and others, especially those humble friends now in so sore a strait, on Him who hath all power in heaven and on earth.

She had tried to lead them to Him. She had talked to them of His love, oftenest to Rachel, being so much more with her, and told them that all wrongs and oppression suffered in this world would be righted in the next, if not here, to those who put their trust in Him and bore patiently with trouble and trial for His sake, quoting to them those comforting words of inspiration, "We know that all things work together for good to them that love God." And also, the words of the Master, "What I do thou knowest not now; but thou shalt know hereafter."

She hoped that those teachings were a help and comfort to them now. She knew their hearts were overwhelmed, and she silently lifted hers in prayer that they might be led to the Rock so much higher than they.

"Hark!" cried Percy suddenly, "I do believe they're coming, mother!" And up he sprang and darted from the room, through the hall, and out the front door.

She threw down her sewing and followed him, her heart beating fast and loud.

"Listen, listen!" he said breathlessly. "That is certainly the creaking of wagon wheels and the tramping of many horses' hoofs. It must be uncle Wallace and his men, and they've brought them back, for they had no wagon with them when they went this morning."

"Yes, and the sounds draw nearer. Oh, how weary, and probably hungry, too, those poor captives must be!" sighed Mildred.

"Don't you believe uncle would see that they had something to eat, mother?" asked the boy.

"Yes, surely. I forgot at that moment that he was of the rescuing party. But keep quiet, son, while they pass," she added in a whisper. "They're almost here."

"You are not afraid, are you, mother?" he asked in an undertone.

"Oh, no, dear child! What is there to fear? But I want to hear any sound they may make—poor, poor things!"

"Here comes father," the boy said, as from the opposite direction a firm, manly step drew near.

"They are coming, Milly, my dear," the doctor said, low and feelingly, as he stepped to her side. "Bill Smith rode into town about ten minutes ago, sent on ahead to bring the news that the kidnappers had been overtaken and compelled to return and prove property.

Mildred made no reply, for with the doctor's last words, the foremost horseman had arrived directly in front of the gate, and she was straining eye and ear to catch sight or sound of the poor fugitives.

But all in vain. The little procession moved past in silence. There were no street lamps, and the stars gave only sufficient light to make the outlines of the passing forms dimly discernible.

When these had vanished and the last echo of the horses' hooves died away down the street, she asked, "What will be done with them tonight, Charlie?"

"I presume Cass will insist that they must be lodged in the jail for safekeeping and watched over by one of his own men."

"Just as if they'd done something wicked!" exclaimed Percy indignantly.

"Doubtless the master considers their running away a crime," replied his father. "And, at all events, he will do his best to prevent their escape."

"Do you think I would be allowed to see and speak to them?" Mildred asked.

"Hardly, if Cass can prevent it. And, on thinking the matter over, it has struck me that the greatest kindness we can now do Sam and Rachel is to keep out of the way of giving enforced testimony that would help their master to prove their identity.

"You remember I knew them in the South, knew that Cass bought Rachel after my uncle's death, and, unfortunately, both you and I were told by her, on her arrival here, that she was his escaped slave."

"Ah, yes!" Mildred said sorrowfully. "Then I will keep away from the poor things, much as I wish for a parting word with them. But I fear Cass will have us summoned to give testimony."

"I hope there is no danger of that," responded her husband, "for I am pretty certain he has not the remotest idea that I am in this part of the Union.

"I must see Wallace before I go to bed. Will you go over with me?"

"The children," Mildred said hesitatingly.

"Are in bed, I know. But we will leave our big boy, Percy, in charge of them and the house."

"Oh, yes, mother, I'll stay and take care of them!" assented the lad with cheerful alacrity.

Wallace was able to assure Mildred that the fugitives were not suffering from cold or hunger but were comfortably lodged in the county jail, and the doctor that, though Cass seemed confident of his ability to prove property in Rachel and her children, and that he was authorized by Sam's master to take him into custody and convey him to his former home, he yet had no suspicion that there was anyone living in that vicinity who would be competent to testify to his ownership.

The parties had the hearing before the judge early the next day, Messrs. Keith and Ormsby acting as counsel for the fugitives, a Mr. Stott, a strong pro-slavery man, for the other side.

The courtroom was crowded, the excitement great.

Ormsby pleaded eloquently in behalf of his poor clients, moving many of his hearers to tears. And Stott, who was a very passionate man, got into such a rage at his denunciations of slavery and those who upheld it—robbing, or helping others to rob, their fellow creatures of the "inalienable right to liberty and the pursuit of happiness"—that he drew out a revolver and, levelling it at Ormsby's head, threatened to blow out his brains on the spot.

At that, the excitement became intense. There were hisses and groans, and many sprang to their feet with cries of:

"Stop him!"

"Take the pistol from him!"

"He ought to be arrested and sent to prison!"

"Down with the bullying rascal!"

"Judge, will you allow that! Are we to have a murder here in open court?"

"Order! Order in the court!" cried the judge. And on the instant all grew quiet, a deep hush succeeding the storm of indignation as they perceived Ormsby was about to speak again.

"Sir," said Wallace, folding his arms and looking the bully calmly in the eye, "that action and the accompanying threat are quite consonant with the spirit of the cause you are upholding, but I fear neither you not it. God helping me, I shall ever stand up for the true and right, the cause of the downtrodden and oppressed, be the personal risk what it may."

He then went on with his plea and was allowed to finish it without further disturbance.

But though on the side of right, the law was against him and his clients, and the slaveholder gained the day.

He made no unnecessary delay after the decision was rendered but instantly hurried his captives into the wagon and away on their southward journey.

Mildred waited at home in a state of half-feverish excitement and distress—waited for, yet half dreaded, Percy's return from the courthouse, where he had been permitted to go with his uncle Rupert.

The time seemed long to her impatience, but at length he came hurrying in, flushed and almost tearful in his sorrow and indignation.

For a moment or two he seemed unable to speak, then he burst out hotly, "Mother, mother, they've gone and given up the poor, hunted creatures to their enemies—the cruel men who treat them as if they were burglars or murderers just because they tried to be free, as everybody has a right to be! The judge and everybody gave them up, and they handcuffed them and tumbled them into that old wagon again, and drove off out of town with them."

"It is just as I feared," Mildred said, the hot tears streaming down her cheeks. "Poor, poor Rachel!"

Percy went on to describe the scene in the courthouse, concluding with, "I was proud of my uncle, mother, and wished there were more such men in the world."

"Yes," she said, "more like him, and many more like your father. It would be a far better and happier world."

The other children had come in from their play time to hear the conclusion of Percy's story. "Oh, Percy, did uncle Wallace get shot?" asked Marcia, in distress.

"No, the fellow had to put up his pistol and keep quiet till uncle had finished his speech."

"And did they let Sam and Rachel go?"

"No, they gave them up to those men, and they've carried them off down South."

"And will we never see them or the children again?"

Percy shook his head sorrowfully.

At that the little ones began to cry, sorry to part from their friends and filled with vague fears on their own account, not being able to understand why white children were in less danger of being carried off than black ones. It took much soothing talk from their mother to comfort them and banish their fears, both then and on subsequent occasions, particularly when they were put to bed at night.

And weeks passed before she could at all forget the sad occurrence or be quite her own, bright, cheerful self again.

The first thing that helped her to a measure of forgetfulness, turning her thoughts into a new and pleasanter channel, was a long letter from her friend and cousin, Mrs. Horace Dinsmore, giving a detailed account of the wedding of Elsie and Mr. Travilla, which had taken place a few days before.

The Keiths, Ormsbys, and Landreths had been invited to attend it, Mildred and Annis most urgently so. But circumstances had prevented, greatly to Elsie's disappointment, as Rose reported in this letter — a most interesting one to the Pleasant Plains relatives, the female portion at least. They had begged that the honeymoon, or part of it, might be spent with them, and so they were somewhat disappointed to learn that the bride and groom had given the preference to Viamede, her birthplace and home of her early infancy.

# CHAPTER VI

THANKSGIVING DAY WAS approaching, and it was to be a glad one for our friends in Pleasant Plains, inasmuch as they looked forward to a reunion of the entire family.

Cyril, now a settled pastor in a neighboring county, was coming home with his wife and babies, and even the missionary sister, Ada, was returning with husband and children from a far-off foreign land to rest and recruit and to see once more the dear parents, now growing old, and the brothers and sisters, over whom so many changes had passed since she went from among them.

This delightful prospect, and the necessity for giving much time and thought to the requisite preparations, helped Mildred greatly in recovering her wonted serenity and cheerfulness.

She was without a servant, for good ones were extremely scarce and poor ones she esteemed worse than none. But she had trained her children to be helpful from the time they were old enough to undertake the simplest duties, and now that Percy had reached the age of ten, and Marcia had entered her ninth year, they were really of more assistance than a majority of those offering themselves for her and who had seen twice their years.

It was far more for their sakes than her own that she had thus trained them. Her husband had at first opposed her on the grounds that he was quite able to hire all needed help and that therefore she was giving herself unnecessary trouble.

"I acknowledge," she said in reply, "that it is more trouble to teach them than to do everything myself, but it is for their good to know how to do such things and also to be educated in habits of industry and the bearing of responsibility. Such training will be worth more to them than a fortune. Money and riches in every other form are easily lost, but good habits not so easily."

"Quite right, my dear," the doctor answered, in his good-humored way. "You shall do just as you please about it. I congratulate myself and them on my having secured so good and wise a mother for my children. And I shall always uphold your authority with my own."

So duties were assigned to Percy and Marcia, little, simple ones at first, other and somewhat more difficult ones as they increased their years and ability.

Mildred had a talent for infusing into her offspring her own cheerful spirit and ennobling motives. She taught them that no honest labor was degrading because God bids us work, and that for our good, for the diligent are far happier than the idle.

Also, that God's eye was ever upon them; that He noticed even little children, their words and ways and motives; that if they performed their appointed tasks patiently, faithfully, and from a desire to please and honor Him, He would know it, He would see that they loved Him and would love them; that He did care for and love them, and wanted them to be happy. And the only way to be happy was to be good, for sin had brought all the sorrow and suffering into the world.

If they complained, as on rare occasions they did, that something that had to be done was distasteful to them, she would say, "Well, dears, we won't stop to think whether we enjoy doing it or not, but will just go on and do it. Then we'll be ready for something we like better." When they did well, she left them in no doubt of her appreciation of their efforts but was liberal with commendation, and she never scolded or fretted over their failures or, indeed, over anything else.

And they esteemed it a pleasure and privilege to "help mother" and their father also, for he was a most kind and indulgent one, and Mildred often took occasion to call their attention to his cares and labors in their behalf.

Percy felt it an honor to be entrusted with the care of the horses and his father's office, the starting of all the fires in winter, the kitchen fire all the year round, and seeing that they were in proper condition for safety through the night. And Marcia was very proud that mother could say that she was as nice a little dishwasher and duster as anybody need desire.

Mildred's rule was, "A place for everything, and everything in its place; a time for everything, and everything in its time." And under her systematic and kindly management, there was seldom any jarring of the domestic machinery—work was comparatively easy, each one knowing and attending quickly to his or her apportioned share of it.

So competent help was employed when it could be had, and when it could not, they cheerfully waited upon themselves and each other, esteeming it no great hardship to be under the necessity of so doing.

Mother and children had a busy, happy time preparing dainties to tempt the appetites of the expected dear ones and making the home as neat and attractive as possible, while the other two families, the Keiths and Ormsbys, were similarly employed.

There would be guests enough for each household to have a share in the joy of entertaining them. All arrived in safety and health at the anticipated time and were most joyfully welcomed.

Don and his family became Mildred's guests; Cyril and his lodged with the Ormsbys; and Ada and her husband and children at her father's, where all the children and grandchildren partook of their Thanksgiving dinner together.

They formed a large party, the older people serenely happy in the reunion, the younger ones full of mirth and jollity.

After dinner the gentlemen fell into earnest discourse on the condition and prospects of the country, the Union of which they were one and all devoted lovers, the Rev. Fran Osborn, the missionary son-in-law, no less than the others, though now breathing his native air for the first time in many years.

It was the fall of '58, the political horizon already darkening with the clouds that burst in so fearful a storm two and a half years later.

"You still consider yourself an American, I suppose, Frank?" remarked Cyril interrogatively.

"Yes, indeed!" he cried.

"I love the dear old Union as fervently as ever, and my desires for her welfare and glory are secondary only to what I entertain for the advancement of Christ's cause and kingdom. From my far-off post, I have been watching with unflagging interest the course of events upon which her destinies seem to hinge, and feeling much anxiety because of threatened danger from the states' rights heresy."

"The prospect does indeed look gloomy in that direction," remarked Rupert. "To grant the right of secession would be to destroy the Union."

"And leave us without a country," added Ormsby.

"The destruction of this great Republic would be a terrible calamity, not to us only but to the world, for it is to her the downtrodden and oppressed of all nations are looking with hope and longing," said the older Mr. Keith.

"I very much fear," sighed the doctor, "that that political heresy is breeding trouble for this land and will bring about a struggle between the sections. There is a hot-blooded element in my native section, who, if they could induce a sufficient number to join with them in the attempt, would be more than willing to whirl their states out of the Union and take up arms for the perpetuation and increase of the power of their leaders."

Percy, overhearing the talk, had left his sports and drawn near the group of gentlemen, his face wearing an intensely interested look, for he was an ardent young patriot.

"Oh, father!" he cried in an eager, excited tone, and coming closer to the doctor's side, said, "do you mean that we may be going to have a war?"

"I mean that there are some mad fellows foolish enough and wicked enough to start one if they could, but I sincerely hope they may never succeed. War, especially civil war, is a terrible thing."

"Well, I hope we won't have one, but if it must come, I hope it won't be till I grow to be a man."

"Why so, Percy?" asked his grandfather.

"Because, if the Union is to be fought for, I want to help fight for it."

"Percy has been reading a great deal about the Revolution of late, and I believe he quite regrets that he hadn't a share in it," remarked his aunt Annis teasingly. "Don't you wish you had been living then, my bonnie laddie?"

"No, auntie, because if I had, I wouldn't be alive now," he answered. "But I do like to read and hear all about those times and the brave men and women that helped to gain freedom for this land."

"Ah? Then I have some stories which will interest you," said his aunt Flora, his uncle Don's wife. "You know our state was a part of the battleground of that war, some very important engagements between the Americans and the British and Tories taking place on her soil."

"Oh, yes!" cried Percy, "I remember that the battles of Monmouth and of Trenton were fought in New Jersey, the battle of Princeton, too. Have you seen those battlefields, Aunt Flora?"

"Yes," she said, "all those and also some places in Pennsylvania that call up Revolutionary memories: Grey's Ferry, Germantown, and Valley Forge."

"How I should like to see them!" exclaimed the boy, his eyes kindling. "Aunt Flora, do you feel like telling those stories now?"

"Don't ask for them today, my son," said Mildred. "Just now almost everyone is more interested in much more recent events. And we expect to keep aunt Flora and uncle Don for a least a week or two."

"Yes, mother, I am sure you are right," responded the lad respectfully and with perfect good humor. "Aunt Flora, please excuse my thoughtlessness in making the request."

"Certainly, Percy," she said, "and you shall have the stories at another time."

Toward bedtime that evening, Mildred was in her kitchen, setting muffins to rise for breakfast, while Percy laid the fire in the cooking stove, ready to light when he should come down in the morning.

"Mother," he said, "I was ashamed of asking aunt Flora for those stories."

"Never mind, you were only a little thoughtless," she returned, smiling affectionately into his blushing, troubled face. "I'll tell you what I have been planning," she went on, "a children's party for you and Marcia, some afternoon while the cousins are here. Do you think you and she would like it?"

"Yes, ma'am, very much indeed, if it will not give you too much trouble."

"No, it need not. You and Marcia can do most of the work of preparing for it and waiting on your little guests while they are here. And after they have had their supper, aunt Flora will perhaps tell those Revolutionary stories for the enjoyment of all."

"Oh, that will be delightful!" he cried with enthusiasm. "Mother, how good you are at planning, and how kind and thoughtful for your children."

"And how happy and fortunate in being so thoroughly appreciated by them," she returned brightly.

A few days later her plan was carried out. All the cousins and a few other intimate friends of her children were invited to assemble in her parlors at an early hour in the afternoon, entertained with innocent games till tea time, then fed upon wholesome dainties. And when their appetites were satisfied, they gathered about "aunt Flor" and listened with much pleasure and interest to her stories of Revolutionary days.

"When I was a little girl," she began, "there lived, not very far from us, a dear little old lady whom everybody called Aunt Sally. She lived by herself in a small house which belonged to her, but that, with the garden around it, was all the property she had.

"All her relatives were gone, too. Her father, mother, brothers, and sisters were all dead, and as she had never married, she had no children.

"She supported herself by knitting, sewing, and doing odd jobs for the neighbors. They would pay her for these, and besides, one or another would often send her some nice eatables, when they happened to have such to spare, or a load of wood to help keep up her fire. So she was quite comfortable.

"She was so good-natured and ready to oblige that she had hosts of friends who were always glad to receive her in their houses, and liked to go to hers and sit and chat with her.

"I was always glad to see her coming to our house and much pleased when sometimes my mother would let me go home with her and stay all night. It was then she used to tell me stories of the Revolutionary War, and I never tired of listening to them.

"She was an old-fashioned body, and she dressed in an odd, old-fashioned way. Her best dress was a chintz with a tea-colored ground and large bunches of bright flowers scattered over it. In my childish eyes, it was extremely handsome.

"As I said, Aunt Sally was quite an old woman when I knew her, but at the time of the Revolution, she was a young girl, and she could tell many things that had happened then.

"She lived at home on her father's farm. He was a Whig; that is, he was for our country and not for the English king who wanted to play the tyrant over it—these colonies, as they were called then, though now they are states.

"So the British and Tories were enemies to Aunt Sally and her family, ready to rob and ill-treat them at every opportunity. And of course, when one day they heard that a party of these enemies were approaching, they made haste to put their valuables out of sight.

"Their horses, which were perhaps their most valuable possessions, except the house and land, and were sure to be taken by the foe if seen, they hid in the cellar, the safest place that could be thought of. But the horses could not be made to understand the necessity for keeping quiet, in case the enemy came near enough to hear their tramping and stamping, so the mother set to work with her spinning wheel, and worked away with as much clatter as possible to drown the noise they were making.

"The British and Tories came in and demanded a meal, but she would not stop her work. She kept on spinning her fastest and bade her young daughters prepare the meal for the soldiers. They did so, and when the men had eaten, they went away without having discovered the horses.

"Another time, Aunt Sally and her sister walked out together to a common at some distance from their home and climbed up into a tree that was growing there to gather its fruit,—probably wild cherries or plums.

"They had not been there very long when they were startled by the sound of a drum and fife in the distance. They knew that meant that the British were coming, and very much frightened they were. They were afraid to stay where they were and equally afraid to get down and try to run away, lest the soldiers should see and pursue them.

"They finally decided to stay in the tree, hoping the soldiers would not happen to look up among its branches as they passed, and so would not know of their vicinity.

"But the next minute, there was another sound which added to their terror: the bellowing of an infuriated bull. The British uniform has so much red about it that the soldiers were commonly called 'redcoats,' and I presume that the sight of it had enraged the bull.

"Presently the girls saw as well as heard him. On he came, snorting, bellowing, pawing the ground, rolling his fiery eyes, and making straight for their tree.

"Oh, how terribly frightened they were! I suppose they shrieked aloud in their terror. At all events, they were discovered by the soldiers. But the officer in command, more kind-hearted and gentlemanly than some others, ordered his men to drive the bull away, and the poor, frightened girls were allowed to get down and run home."

"Is that all, Aunt Flor?" asked Marcia.

"Yes, my dear, all of that one."

"Oh, please tell some more of Aunt Sally's stories!" pleaded several young voices.

"That is all I can recall just now of her stories,"

said Mrs. Keith, "but I can tell you some incidents of that time which occurred in South Carolina.

"They were told me by a lady whose grandfather, General White, was in Charleston during the Revolution and there fell in love with a young girl, whom he afterwards married.

"An older sister of that young lady behaved in a very spirited manner toward the British while they held the city.

"When they took possession, several of the officers were quartered upon her, she being a young lady of wealth and standing.

"One of the officers coolly took her bedroom for his own use, putting out all her clothing and other feminine articles.

"She ordered him to give it up, saying, 'I am a lady. The room is mine, and you must content yourself with some other.'

"'I will not,' he answered insolently. 'You will have to content yourself with another. Anything is good enough for rebels.'

"'I shall complain to your commanding officer,' she replied, setting off at once for his quarters and taking her little sister with her.

"When she arrived there and asked for an interview, his subordinates refused her admission to his presence, saying that he was at dinner and must not be disturbed.

"'I will wait,' she said, setting herself, and she did wait for a long while.

"At length he came into the room, expressed surprised on seeing her, said he would not have kept a lady waiting so long if he had known it, and asked what she wanted.

"She explained.

66

"He said, 'That man shall be removed, and I will send you a gentleman.'

"She went home well pleased with the result of her effort and, arriving there, found the obnoxious officer just taking his departure in a great rage, cursing and swearing.

"But the one sent in his place was a gentleman. He treated his hostess with politeness, and whenever news of a British victory was received — knowing that her house would be illuminated in honor of it, and that that would hurt her feelings — he would advise her to go into the country for a while, then light it up while she was absent."

"He must have been pretty nice for a Briton," remarked Percy. "But is that all that lady told you, auntie?"

"I fear you are tiring aunt Flora," remonstrated his mother.

"Oh, no! It is a theme I am fond of," Mrs. Keith said pleasantly.

"I remember a few more incidents.

"An old lady living in the country, somewhere in that region, had a rather singular experience.

"She was in her own room one day when a servant came running to her in great affright, saying, 'The British are coming! They'll be here directly and will rob us of everything we have! Oh, what shall we do?'

"The old lady opened her Bible, and casting her eye on a text that says, 'Thine eye shall not see thine enemy,' she said, 'I shall not see them.'

"'But how can you help it?' she was asked. 'They will be here directly and will ransack the whole house.'

"'I shall not see them,' she repeated, and she did

not. They came and pillaged the rest of the house but did not open her door, though it was merely latched.

"Another woman, large and fat, went to bed when she heard the British were coming to her home, and she put her money under her.

"They ordered her to get up, but she would not.

"They turned up the bed—now on this side, now on that,—but did not find her money.

"Now, I have just one more little anecdote to tell. A Charleston belle was much admired by a British officer but would have nothing to do with him. One day, meeting her in the street, he called out to a big Negro near at hand, 'Come here, fellow! Come and kiss this lady, and I'll give you a golden guinea.'

"You see, she would none of his kisses, and he thought to be revenged on her, supposing she would think it far worse to be kissed by a Negro. But she turned toward the black man, saying, 'Yes, come and kiss me. I'd a thousand times rather be kissed by you than by him.'"

"He must have felt quite mortified that she preferred that fellow to him," remarked one of the girls, laughing.

"And it served him just right," commented Percy.

# CHAPTER VII

AS TIME PASSED on and Percy grew in both stature and intellect, his interest in all that concerned the welfare of his country seemed to deepen. He had a keen appetite for information, particularly on that subject, read all he could find on it in books and newspapers, and asked many questions of father, grandfather, and uncles—his mother, also, for he had the greatest respect for her attainments and her judgment of affairs.

The presidential campaign of 1860 interested and excited him very much, and he used his best efforts in favor of the Republican candidates, because his father, grandfather, and uncles all belonging to that party, he naturally thought it the best and that in helping it, he was forwarding the cause of his country.

To be sure, he had no vote (though his knowledge of our institutions, his intellect, and general information were far in advance of those of multitudes of foreigners who had) and no great amount of influence, but all that he had he threw upon that which he deemed the right side.

He had become an acknowledged leader among his mates, and he exerted all his influence to make them as patriotic as himself, talking to them singly

or haranguing them in groups, repeating the sub-
stance of what he had learned from his older
friends or gleaned from the editorials and speeches
in the newspapers he had been reading.

He came rushing into the house one November
day, into the sitting room where his mother was
busily sewing and his father, just returned from a
long, cold ride into the country, was standing
before the fire, warming himself.

"Hello!" cried the doctor, catching sight of his
boy's radiant face. "So Lincoln's elected!"

"Yes, sir," cried the lad, his eyes sparkling with
delight, "and I though I'd be the first to tell the
good news to you and mother, but it seems you had
heard it before."

"No, I learned it from you," laughed the doctor.
"One glance at your face was quite sufficient,
knowing your politics as I do."

"Yes, sir, and aren't you glad, too, father?"

"I am not sorry," the doctor replied, but with a
sigh and a slight clouding of his usually cheerful
countenance. "I certainly did not want the other
side to win—and yet the outlook for our country is
not, to say the least, a very bright one at present."

"What is it you fear for her, Charlie?" asked his
wife. And Percy listened anxiously for the reply.

"Further contention between the sections, perhaps an attempt to secede on the part of some of
the Southern states. In fact, I have little doubt that
that will be the outcome. You know it has been
threatened, so I can see scarce a hope of escape
from the dismemberment of our great, glorious old
Union unless through the horrors of civil war
resulting in victory for the government."

"Oh, I—I do not know how to believe my

countrymen can be so mad as to go to war with each other, and the very idea absolutely terrifies me!" cried Mildred in a tone, and with a look, of keen distress. "Just to think, for instance, of my brothers here and our relatives down South killing each other! Oh, how horrible!"

"It would be, indeed," he said with emotion. "May God in his great mercy avert such a calamity! It is our strong consolation, dear wife, that He rules and reigns. 'The Lord is great in Zion; and He is high above all the people.'"

"Yes," she said, "'God is our refuge and strength, a very present help in trouble. Therefore will we not fear, though the earth be removed, and though the mountains be carried into the midst of the sea.'" Thus they stayed themselves upon the God of Israel, and found much peace in so doing, in spite of the gathering storm that, but for this strong refuge, would have filled their hearts with dismay and despair. For a very short time brought the fulfillment of the doctor's fears, the election being made the pretext for secession and rebellion by one after another of the cotton states, South Carolina leading the way on the 20th of the next month, the others following in rapid succession.

What was to be the end of it? The great Republic seemed falling to pieces. Would this destruction of the grand work of our Revolutionary fathers be allowed to go on unhindered? Were their sons made of so much less sterner stuff that they would not lift a hand to preserve it, that glorious heritage bought for them with so much flood and toil? The questions were warmly discussed by men and women—even by boys and girls, also—in their homes, in shops, stores, and streets: everywhere.

*Martha Finley*

One afternoon Mr. Rupert Keith, passing along a common soon after the schools had closed for the day, noticed Percy mounted on a stump and earnestly haranguing a crowd of boys who seemed to be listening in rapt attention.

Rupert smiled at the sight and quickened his steps, desiring to get near enough to hear what the lad was saying.

But the first thing he heard was an interruption from one of the crowd.

"I say! My pap says they've a right to go if they want ter, and they'd orter be let go peaceable."

"No, sir!" exclaimed Percy emphatically. "It wouldn't do at all, for if one has a right to go, all have the same right. And if we acknowledge that, one state may drop off after another till there won't be two left together to make a Union, and we'd be without a country. One state by itself wouldn't be worth calling a country.

"And if the states may secede from the Union, the counties may secede from the states, and the towns from the counties. And what would be the end of it? Probably that we'd all take to fighting among ourselves, and there'd be a worse war than we'll have if the federal government undertakes to make these rebellious states stay in the Union."

Cries of "That's so! You're right, Landreth!" came from a number of voices in the crowd. And Mr. Keith passed on, smiling to himself in a pleased way, thinking that his nephew was a lad of promise, bidding fair to be a credit to the family.

He had no children of his own but was proud and fond of those of his brothers and sisters.

That evening he went into Dr. Landreth's to

72

have a chat with him and Mildred, and finding Percy in the sitting room with his parents, rallied him good-humoredly on his efforts as a stump-speaker. "You are becoming a politician and an orator," he said. "We'll have you running for Congress one of these days, or perhaps even for the presidency."

"I don't know about that, uncle," said the boy, coloring, "but I'd rather be a patriot than a politician. I'd rather be a nobody in a glorious, free country than hold the highest office—even be absolute monarch—in one where the people were downtrodden and oppressed."

"That's right! I'm proud of you, my boy," his uncle responded, clapping him on the shoulder. "If all the lads would cherish such sentiments and act upon them, we might feel sure of a glorious future for our country."

"As probably they would if all the mothers were like his," remarked the doctor with a glance of fond, proud affection at this wife.

"Yes," assented Rupert, "mothers have a vast deal to do with the formation of the characters of their sons and daughters."

"Fathers, too," said Mildred, returning her husband's glance with an equally appreciative one. "If my boy has any admirable qualities, he does not get them all from me."

"No," assented her brother, "I know he owes a good deal to having a good father, too, and also generations of God-fearing ancestors."

Then, turning to the doctor, he said, "What do you think of the news of today from Texas: Twiggs's surrender of United States forces and military stores to the state?"

"A dastardly piece of business but quite in keeping with other acts of the Rebels."

"Wasn't it stealing?" asked Percy. "I mean for the state to take them?"

"Just as much as for a man in a business partnership to take and use as his own any property belonging to the firm," replied his uncle. "Look, too, at the ingratitude of an officer educated by the United States government turning against her and using the very knowledge and skill he owes to her in attempting her destruction!"

"Yes, that is all true," said the doctor. "And yet I can readily see how a man may find the question of whether his allegiance belongs primarily to his state or to the general government a difficult one to decide."

"Yes, I suppose it may be to men educated from infancy to look upon their state as their country. But we who have always been taught that our country is the United States find no such difficulty."

"Oh!" cried Mildred. "Must it come to war? I cannot yet believe that it will. The very thought is so dreadful!"

"It looks more and more like it," said Rupert. "War is a dreadful, dreadful thing, especially war between brethren, but there are some alternatives which are even worse. Would it not be worse to stand passively by and see this grand Republic, this country which we proudly call our own and justly regard with strongest affection, go to pieces, rent asunder and destroyed by her own recreant sons? Would it not be worse to surrender to the attacks of traitors the liberties bought for us and generations yet unborn by the blood and toil of our Revolutionary fathers? What right have we to give up tamely the rights and privileges they secured for us and our posterity at such a cost?"

"I don't think we have any," cried Percy warmly, "and I only wish I was old enough to help, if there's to be a fight. But what are they waiting for? Why doesn't the government begin at once to make these seceding states come back?"

"Ah, my son, it is often much easier to ask questions than to answer them," replied the doctor.

"I'm thinking," remarked Rupert, "that if our present chief magistrate had the courage and grit of old Andrew Jackson, things would not have been allowed to come to such a pass without at least an effort to bring treason and traitors to punishment."

"I am glad his term of office has so nearly expired," said Mildred. "But do you gentlemen think there will be any effort on the part of the disaffected to prevent Mr. Lincoln's inauguration?"

Both husband and brother answered in the affirmative. It was feared, they said, that there might be an attempt to assassinate him.

"It must be a bad cause that needs to be upheld by such crimes," she said. "But if, as I truly believe, God has raised him up for this very time, as he did Washington for the Revolution, he will escape them. 'Man is immortal till his work is done.'"

# CHAPTER VIII

WEARILY THE WEEKS and months dragged by, the political horizon still growing darker, though the cloud seems slow to burst. It was as if the nation, the loyal part of it, held its breath in expectation. The inauguration was safely past and Mr. Lincoln in occupancy of the White House, but the poisonous leaven of treason continued to work. The South was in a ferment; the North seemed half paralyzed with amazement at her madness, incredulous of the fact, growing daily more apparent, that she meant to inaugurate a fratricidal war, since by no other means might she rule in the nation's counsels and force her "peculiar institution" upon new states and territories.

But the half-benumbed North was aroused as by an electric shock when the news flashed over the wires: "Fort Sumter has fallen after a terrific bombardment of thirty-six hours!"

So the first blow had been struck! The dread issue was upon her! The Union was lost unless she arose in her might for its salvation, the flag forever dishonored should she refuse to step forward it its defense! The flag! That beautiful star-spangled banner! She had not known, she had not dreamed how dear it was to her heart. But now that it had been insulted and trampled in the dust, and that by those to whom it should have been as dear as to herself, what a furor of love to it, and indignation against them, swept from ocean to ocean and from north to south within her borders!

Everywhere it was flung to the breeze with a wondrous fervor of patriotic love and loyalty, with speeches and songs in its praise. The soul-stirring strains of *Hail Columbia*, *Yankee Doodle*, and *The Star Spangled Banner*, but especially the last, were heard on all sides and at almost all hours, played by brass bands and sung by the voices of men, women, and children. The enthusiasm was astonishing and as strongly displayed at Pleasant Plains as anywhere else.

"Mother, mother, we must have a flag!" cried the children—Percy, Marcia, and Stuart—rushing in from school. "They've got one on the courthouse, and one's to be put on the schoolhouse this afternoon. Oh!" she said, catching sight of her, their grandmother, and two aunts, all at work upon red, white, and blue materials, "you're making one?"

"Yes, dears. This is for grandpa's house, and we intend to make two others as fast as we can, one for your uncle Wallace's and the other for our own."

"And each one is to be run up with speech and songs," said their aunt Annis in her lively way. "So, Percy, set to work and prepare your speech. Perhaps, though, you are so full of patriotic love for the old flag, and indignation at the Rebels who have dared to treat it with such contempt, that you need no preparation, words coming to your lips as fast as you can utter them."

"I think such an occasion should be honored by a good deal better speaker, uncle Wallace, for instance," returned Percy modestly. "I only talk to the boys, auntie."

"But he can talk ever so well. I've heard him often, so I know," Marcia said, looking proudly at her brother.

"It's so," asserted Stuart stoutly. "I've heard him, too. And Stuart Ormsby and all the boys say he's a first-rate speaker."

"I'm glad to hear that my boy is so ready to acknowledge his cousin's talents," remarked their aunt Zillah, glancing up from her work with a pleasant smile. "Where is he, boys?"

"Just coming in at the gate," said little Fan Landreth, who was standing in the doorway. "And he's got a great big bundle in his arms."

"What's that, Stuart?" asked his mother as the boy came in.

"Some stuff to make a flag," he answered, hastily undoing his package and displaying its contents. "I went to father's office and told him we ought to have one on our house, and he said I might go to the store and get the stuff, and he'd no doubt you'd be willing enough to make it."

"Yes, but I had already bought material for one. You should have consulted me first."

"Well, can't we have two?" he asked. "It wouldn't hurt if we had a dozen."

"It might hurt your mother—wear her out to some extent—to make so many," laughed aunt Annis.

"But we can help! Can't we all help?" cried Marcia eagerly.

"I don't think you can, dears," said their grandmother. "You see, your mother and I are basting, and your aunt Zillah and aunt Annis are running the machines, and really, we are as many as can work on them at once."

"I might take my turn at running the sewing machine," said Percy. "You know, mother, you say I can do that quite well."

"Yes, so you can," she answered. "And whenever either of your aunts wants a rest, I think you may be called upon to help in that."

"But why can't we make this other flag?" queried Stuart Ormsby a little impatiently.

"Oh, I know what we can do!" cried Percy, clapping his hands. "We can make it for the house of Sam and Rachel used to live in. We children, I mean. Oh, mother, mother, can't we?"

"Yes, if I may pay for the materials," she said, "looking at Mrs. Ormsby.

"You may pay half, if you prefer to do so," Zillah said, "but not more, as my boy is to have half the fun."

"No, no, mother, not more than quarter!" spoke up her own little daughter Ada, "because Mar and I are going to share it with the boys. S'pose girls can't help with the fighting, if there's to be any. Percy says they can't, but we'll do our share of the sewing, won't we, Mar?"

"Yes," said Marcia, "and I think it would be nice to make some little flags to put over our front gates."

"There's no school this afternoon," announced Stuart Ormsby. "Everybody's going to be busy making flags and putting them up on the houses." He was spreading the contents of his package on the carpet as he spoke.

"Do you think you children can cut your flag out for yourselves?" asked Mildred.

"Yes, ma'am. The stripes will be easy enough for anybody. It'll only be to measure the width and tear them off, won't it?"

"Yes, but the stars you will find more difficult."

"Yes, ma'am, but I can cut them if I have a pattern, and I'll look at one of your flags to see where to tack them on."

"I think Stuart can do it," his mother said, "with a little help from one of us older people, if not without."

"At any rate, he may as well try," remarked his grandmother. "There's nothing like trying. Here's a pattern for you to cut the stars by. You can cut a few out, Stuart, while Percy measures and tears off the red and white strips. Your blue ground is all ready, I see. Then he can begin tacking the stars onto it while you go on cutting out the rest."

"Yes, ma'am," they said, setting to work at once with great zeal.

"And what can we girls do grandma?" asked Marcia disconsolately.

"Make the little flags for the gates that you were talking of," she replied, taking out her purse. "I'll give you some money, and you can run to the store and ask for enough material to make two flags about a yard long."

"Oh, thank you, grandma, thank you!" they cried in chorus, starting off at once.

All that afternoon and evening, and part of the next day—except when irresistibly attracted by the ceremonies of a nearby flag-raising—the children worked with unabated zeal, energy, and industry.

At last, with exultation and delight, they announced that their task was finished. The large flag undertaken by Stuart and Percy, and the little ones of their sisters, were completed almost simultaneously.

Those made by the older people had been already flung to the breeze, one over the front entrance of each dwelling, and were waving in it now.

All the public buildings and very many private ones were similarly adorned, and not a jot of the furor for the beautiful emblem of our nationality had abated.

"We're done! We're done! Our flags are all finished!" cried the children in Mildred's sitting room in rejoicing chorus.

"Aren't they handsome, mother?" exclaimed Percy, rubbing his hands in delight as he stood gazing at them with fond, admiring eyes. "Somehow they look even prettier to me than any of the others in town."

"To me, too!" chimed in Stuart Ormsby.

"Because of the painstaking labor you have put into them," Mildred said. "We value more highly that which has cost us some exertion in the obtaining."

"Yes, I have always found it so," responded Percy with the air of one who has many years. "Now for the raising of this big fellow. I told all the boys to come round about three o'clock to help at it. And," he said, glancing at the face of the tall clock ticking in the hall, "it wants only ten minutes of the time."

"And look, the fellows are beginning to come," said Stuart, turning toward the window. "There are half a dozen of them at the gate. Got your speech ready?"

"Oh, yes. It'll only be a few words about the old flag, how we should love it, resent the insult that had been offered it, and be ready to fight for it to our last gasp, rather than see it trampled in the dust. Because in fighting for it, we would be fighting for our country, fighting to save the Union."

They hastily caught up their hats, then the flag, and, carrying it between them, passed out into the street and round by the lane to the front of the small dwelling at the foot of the garden, Stuart Landreth following and their schoolmates joining them as they issued from the gate.

"Mother, mother, may we go too? May we, Aunt Mildred?" the little girls were asking.

"We will go through the garden into the house," Mildred answered. "It is not occupied just now, you know, and I will open a front window so that we can see and hear all that goes on without getting into the crowd of boys."

"You've never heard one of Percy's speeches, have you, mother?" asked Marcia as they hurried on their way.

"No, dear, and I have some curiosity to do so," Mildred answered with a little amused laugh.

They found both back and front doors open and Percy mounted on a chair just outside the latter, one end of the flag thrown over his left arm and shoulder, and Stuart Ormsby supporting the other end, keeping it carefully up out of the dust. The rest of the boys gathered in a little crowd in front of them.

The orator of the day was beginning, "Fellow citizens," he said, as his mother came within hearing.

She held up her finger in warning to the lads facing her, signed to the little girls to keep quiet, and with them stood listening till Percy had finished.

His address was, as he had said it would be, only a few words of love and loyalty to the flag and the Union, and of denunciation of the traitors who had dared to fire upon the one and attempt the destruction of the other. There was applause as he closed.

"Hurrah for the Union! Hurrah for the old flag! Hurrah for Landreth!"

"Thank you, lads," he said. "Now we'll put up our flag, and then we'll have *The Star Spangled Banner* sung with a will."

"How are you going to get it up?" asked a voice from the crowd.

"We have a stout cord through it, don't you see? Stuart Ormsby will climb that tree yonder and tie one end to a branch while I get out on the roof and fasten the other round the chimney."

"And we're all ready to help," responded several voices eagerly.

"Mother, I didn't know you were here!" cried Percy, turning round.

"I wanted to hear what my boy had to say for his country and her flag," she said. "Be careful, in going on the roof, that you don't slip and fall."

"Yes, ma'am, I will. I've been on it often, though. Father knows and has never forbidden me."

"No, nor do I; only be careful." But she waited anxiously till he came down again, his boyish voice singing loudly, in unison with those of his mates:

> *"That star-spangled banner,*
> *Oh, long may it wave!"*

"Now Percy, please come and put up our flags," called Marcia as the last strain died away.

"Yes, sis, we will," he answered heartily. "Come

on, boys, but if there's to be a speech, somebody else must make it. I haven't anything more to say."

"I'll do that part," promised his little brother, straightening himself with an air of importance.

"I wonder what my little Stuart can find to say," laughed Mildred. "It will be your maiden speech, won't it, my boy?"

"I don't know what that means, mother," he said, looking somewhat abashed.

"The first."

"Yes, ma'am, I never have tried yet."

"This flag-raising won't be much," Percy said to his mates as they hurried round through the lane again. "There are just two tiny flags fastened to a staff, and nailing them to the gate posts is all there'll be of it."

"Well, that'll be easy enough, and we want to hear little Stuart's speech," they said.

"I'm not going to make up anything; I can't till I'm older," said the little boy. "I'm only going to speak a bit of a piece I've learned, like we do at school."

"Well, here we are," said his cousin Stuart. "Where'll you stand?"

"On the top step of the porch."

Taking his station there, and gesticulating with his small right hand," he shouted,

> *"'Strike for your altars and your fires!*
> *Strike for the green graves of your sires,*
> *God, and your native land.'"*

There was a general laugh, and someone called out, "What's that got to do with the flag, sonny?"

"I guess it's what we've got to do, if we mean to

stop the Rebs from insulting it," returned the little fellow stoutly. "So I thought it would suit tolerably well."

"Yes," his mother said, repressing an inclination to smile, "it will do very well. Now Percy, nail the flags to the posts, and then we'll have *The Star Spangled Banner* again."

# CHAPTER IX

TWO DAYS LATER Percy came hurrying in from the telegraph office, where he had been before breakfast, so eager was he, in common with all the rest, for news.

He looked a little pale, Mildred thought as she glanced at his face, and there was a sort of subdued excitement in his manner.

"Mother," he said in an awestruck tone, "it has come!"

"What my son?" she asked, though only too well she knew.

"War, mother. The President calls for seventy-five thousand men to put down the rebellion in the cotton states. Where's my father?"

"In bed—and asleep, I hope. He didn't get there till long past midnight."

"He won't have to go, mother, will he?"

"Go where?" she asked, her cheek paling, her lips a little tremulous.

"To the war?"

"I—I don't know. I hardly think so. I don't see how he could be spared by his patients."

"Or his wife and children." said Percy.

"Ah, no!" she sighed. "But other men have wives and children, too, and there's no reason why he should be exempt from sacrificing everything on the altar of our common country more than they."

"They wouldn't take a boy like me, would they, mother?"

"No, surely not. The call is for men."

"Oh, if I were only a man!" he exclaimed. "But I'm afraid it will be all over before I am."

"Afraid? Oh, Percy! How rejoiced I should be to know that it would not last a month!"

"I wonder what they are saying about it at grandpa's and uncle's?"

"About what, Percy?" asked Marcia, coming from the parlor, duster in hand.

"The news. War is to begin really. The President has called for troops—seventy-five thousand men—to stop the rebellion."

"Oh, has he? Mother, will father have to go?"

"I cannot tell much about it yet, dear, but I think busy physicians are not likely to be the first," Mildred answered in low, troubled tones. "Besides," she added the next moment, "if he should go, it would be as a surgeon to minister to the sick and wounded, and he would not be in so much danger as the fighting men."

"And grandpa's too old?" Marcia said, half inquiringly.

"Oh, yes!" her mother answered, "but—your uncles are not. Did you see them when you were out, Percy?"

"Yes, ma'am. uncle Rupert and uncle Wallace were both in the crowd about the telegraph office, so they must have heard the news. But they were busy talking, and I didn't wait to speak to them."

"I'm done with my dusting, mother," said Marcia.

"Yes, dear. You may put your duster in its place, then go softly upstairs and listen at the bedroom door for any sound your father may be making. If all is quiet, don't go in to disturb him, but if you hear him moving about, knock and tell him breakfast is ready."

"What can I do to help you, mother?" Percy asked as Marcia left the room. "I see you have butter cakes mixed. May I bake them?"

"Yes, after your father comes down. You can do it quite as nicely as I," she added, smiling affectionately upon him.

"And it is a great pleasure to help you, mother," he said, flushing with gratification at her praise. "Perhaps I might enlist as a cook. Would you give me a recommendation?"

"My dear boy, it is too serious a subject for jest," sighed Mildred.

Just then the front door was heard to open. A quick, light step came through the hall and on into the kitchen where they were.

"Annis! Good morning," Mildred said.

"Good morning, Milly. You've heard the news, I suppose!" exclaimed the young girl, dropping half breathlessly into a chair, "that the President calls for troops?"

"Yes. Oh, Annis, it seems it is to be war after all! I could not believe it before."

"Yes, but some think it will be over in three months. I suppose the President is of that opinion, since his call is for enlistments for only that length of time."

"I hope they may not be mistaken. Still, a great many men may be killed and maimed in ninety days' time."

"And Rupert says he will go," cried Annis, bursting into a storm of tears. "He thinks he should be one of the first to offer, as he is strong and healthy, has no children, and can leave his wife well provided for if—if he shouldn't come back."

Stuart and Fan came running in, announcing that they had finished the work expected of them before breakfast—sweeping off porches and pavements, and weeding their shares of the garden. But they broke off suddenly to ask, with concern, what mother and aunt Annis were crying about.

"War," returned Percy, sententiously, for to him their query had been addressed in an awed whisper.

"Oh, has it come?" asked Stuart.

But Percy did not answer, their father and Marcia joining them at that moment.

"Good morning, wife, sister, children," the doctor said in his usual cheery tones. "Milly, love, and Annis, don't be so distressed. This thing may not last long. We will hope to see it over in a few weeks, or months at the farthest."

"But Rupert answers this call," sobbed Annis. "They have raised a company already and chosen him captain, though he volunteered as a private. And they will start for Washington tonight or tomorrow."

"Poor mother and Juanita!" said Mildred, in tremulous tones. "How do they bear it?"

"Mother looks very pale and sad, but she says, 'Go, if you feel that you ought. I will not refuse any or all my sons to my country in her hour of need.' Juanita weeps but does not try to dissuade her husband. She would not have him a coward, she says, or wanting in love to his native land, but she begs to go with him, so that if he would be sick or wounded, she may be at hand to nurse him back to health."

"And she is an accomplished nurse," remarked the doctor. "I never saw a better."

"You haven't been to breakfast yet, I see," said Annis, rising as if to go.

"No, but can't you stay and eat with us?" asked her brother and sister.

"No, thank you. I can't eat, and I've been through the form of breakfasting already."

"Stay and talk, then," suggested the doctor.

"No, thank you again," she said. "I must go home and see what I can do to help get Rupert ready. There's very little time for it, you see."

"Tell mother I'll be over directly after breakfast," Mildred said, calling after her sister as she went out, "and ready to help in anyway that I can."

"I wonder what our Dinsmore cousins will do?" said Percy as if thinking aloud.

"You remember cousin Horace and his family, cousin Elsie and hers, are in Europe," said his mother. "And very glad of it they must be, for surely it would go hard with cousin Horace or Mr. Travilla to fight on either side."

"No doubt of it. It certainly would with me," said the doctor.

"Then you are not going, father?" queried Percy, looking unmistakably glad.

"Not yet. I cannot see that it is my duty to leave my work here at present. And if I go at all, it will be not be to fight but to care for and help the wounded on both sides."

"Yes, sir. I'm glad of that. Somebody must do that part, and I believe you know how better than most anybody else. But," he added thoughtfully, "somebody's got to fight—yes, a good many somebodies must, or the Union will be lost, all broken up."

"True," said his father. "Nor will men for that work be wanting. And the day will come when those who are now so madly trying to break it up will thank them for saving it."

"The secessionists seem actually crazed now, but they will come to their senses by and by."

"How soon, Charlie?" asked his wife, fixing mournful eyes upon his face.

"That I cannot tell, my dear, but we will try to hope it may be in a few weeks," he answered with forced cheerfulness.

"I think," he went on, "that the greatest sufferers in this struggle will be the loyal people in the South. I have no doubt there are hundreds and thousands there who love the Union and the told flag quite as well as we do. And how terrible it must be to them to be swept along with this current of rebellion against their will!"

"Indeed it must!" said Mildred. "My heart aches for them."

"Mother," spoke up little Fan, "can't God help them, and take care of them? And shan't we ask Him to?"

"Yes, daughter, we will ask Him, and we know that He is able to help all His creatures, no matter where they are or in what trouble."

"And the Bible tells us that God is the hearer and answerer of prayer," added the doctor, "and He says, 'Call upon me in the day of trouble: I will deliver thee, and thou shalt glorify me.' And of the man who gives himself to His service and puts his trust in Him, He says, 'He shall call upon me, and I will answer him: I will be with him in trouble; I will deliver him, and honor him.'"

They did not linger long over their meal. Family prayers followed immediately after.

"Mother," Percy said when they had risen from their knees, "you want to go to grandpa's. We children will put the things away and wash the dishes. Won't we, Mar? We can do it all before school time, if we hurry."

"Yes, of course we can. Please, mother, let us," said Marcia.

"And Fan and I'll help," said Stuart.

"Course we will," added Fan, heartily.

"That's right, children," said their father, "the work won't hurt you. Milly, my dear, I'll go over with you and learn what are the plans and arrangements."

They found a busy household.

Zillah was there before them and met them at the door with the announcement, "A telegram has just come from Don. He has enlisted, too. Juanita will not consent to be left behind, and the plan now is for her to go on with Rupert as far as Philadelphia, then to New Jersey, and stay with Flora till Rupert can see if he can arrange in any way to have her nearer him."

"A very good plan," said the doctor. "She will then be near enough to reach her husband quickly in case he needs her nursing at any time."

"And I think she is quite right to insist upon going," added Mildred.

They passed on into the sitting room where the elder Mrs. Keith sat sewing on a garment belonging to the son about to leave her for the defense of his country and to meet the dangers and uncertainties of war.

Her face was pale and sad but perfectly calm.

"Dearest mother, how well you bear it," Mildred said low and feelingly, leaning down over her to press a tender kiss upon the still-fresh cheek.

"If I do, dear daughter," said the sweet voice that was always music in the ears of husband and children, "it is because I find Him faithful to His promise, 'As thy days, so shall thy strength be.' And well I know that nothing can befall without His will. Let us cast all our care upon Him — care for our dear ones and for our dear native land."

"Yes, mother, there is no comfort, no peace, to be obtained in any other way. It seems as if this may be the time Jesus spoke of when He said there should be 'upon the earth distress of nations, with perplexity; the sea and the waves roaring; men's hearts failing them for fear, and for looking after those things which are coming on the earth.'"

"Yes, but 'a Man shall be as an hiding place from the wind, and a covert from the tempest; as rivers of water in a dry place, as the shadow of a great rock in a weary land.' He is a strong refuge whereunto we may continually resort."

"Wallace has not enlisted, Zillah?" the doctor said inquiringly.

"No, not yet. But he is raising a company to be ready for the next call, should there be another."

"And you are willing?"

"More than willing! I could not withhold my best and dearest from my country in her hour of need. I would go myself if I were a man, or the work such as women might undertake."

"You are very patriotic," he said. And turning toward his wife, he added, "I think Mildred is no less so."

"Oh, Charlie," Zillah hastened to say, "somebody must stay at home, and I hope you are not thinking of going, for what could we do without you? Just suppose that father or mother or one of the children should be taken very sick. I, for one, should be in sore distress, for there is not another doctor in town in whom I feel any confidence."

"I think your place is here Charlie," said his father-in-law. "You have a large practice and really can't be spared—at least not while there are so many thousands who can be spared so much more easily."

"You are all very kind to put so high an estimate upon my services," he said. "I think, however, my place would soon be supplied, at least if it were understood that I was gone permanently. For I have often noticed that, no matter how necessary a man may seem in the place he fills, when death calls him away, his niche is quickly occupied and his work taken up by another, so that soon he is scarcely missed except by those to whom he was very near and dear."

"Yes, that is very true," Mr. Keith acknowledged. "Still, we must keep our doctor with us if we can."

It was a very busy time with the women, not only of this family connection but of the town, till the company left for Washington.

The sorrow of the parting from husbands, fathers, sons, brothers going into the deadly conflict to risk life and limb for the salvation of their native land, who can describe?

But time must not be wasted in idle lamentation while so much work remained for willing hands to do. A Ladies' Aid Society was speedily formed, for the men in the field must be clothed and hospital supplies provided for the sick and wounded.

Some measured and cut out garments, some made their needles fly in basting them together, while others kept the sewing machines humming from morning to night. Knitting needles, too, were set to work, for the soldiers must have warm woolen stockings. Girls—and even boys—engaged in this occupation and in scraping lint and preparing bandages.

Percy, Marcia, and Stuart Landreth, and Stuart and Ada Ormsby also, soon became actively engaged in these latter employments and also did more to help with home duties, so that their mothers might have the more leisure to work for the soldiers.

It was a time of intense activity to those disposed to make themselves useful to the cause of the Union, and of a dreadful kind of excitement, almost every day bringing news that fed either their hopes or fears. And, if the former, they were raised, only to be dashed to the ground again, almost immediately.

How awful, how heart rending, seemed the tidings of the first actual bloodshed: the killing of Massachusetts troops passing through Baltimore on their way to respond to the President's call! So terrible, because it was the first! Alas! It was but a very slight foretaste of that which was to follow.

The doctor brought Mildred this news.

"What a singular coincidence that it occurred on the anniversary of the battle of Lexington, in which the first blood of the Revolution was shed," he remarked. "And that in this instance, as in that, it was the blood of Massachusetts men and the first of the war."

"Yes," she said, "and if I believed in omens, I should say that it was probably a good one. The cause of right, justice, and liberty prevailed in that struggle, and so will they in this. Charlie, I have hardly a doubt that the government will win in the end, though, alas, it may have to be through seas of blood. And oh, how dreadful, how dreadful it is to think that our countrymen are actually engaged in shedding each other's blood!"

"Yes," he sighed, "and I grow daily less hopeful that the struggle will be of short duration. But, like you, I have little doubt that the government will win finally."

Her needle flew as they talked.

"How very industrious you are," he remarked admiringly. "Something for the soldiers, as usual, I suppose?"

"Yes. I am basting shirts ready for the machine, and Percy will be in presently to run it for me. Charlie, I do really think we may be excused if we are a trifle proud of our children, for they are so obedient, affectionate, and industrious, so anxious to do all they can now for the country.

"I accidentally overheard a talk between them the other day.

"They were scraping lint, even Fan trying her little hand at it.

"The first thing I heard was Marcia's voice saying, in an earnest tone, 'Oh, I do wish I could do something really worthwhile to help save the Union! But aren't we doing a little, Percy, in making this lint and knitting the stockings?'

"'Yes,' he said, 'and in saving mother's time and strength so that she can do more. And she does help, making such piles of things for the soldiers!'

"'But all that we children can do seems so very little,' Marcia said, a trifle disconsolately.

"Then Percy spoke again in his bright, cheery tones that were so like his father's," he said, and Mildred smiled up into her husband's face.

"'That needn't discourage you, sis, for you must remember that thousands besides ourselves are at work in the same way, and altogether we'll accomplish a great deal, just as

> *"'Little drops of water, little grains of sand,*
> *make the mighty ocean and the beauteous land.'*

"And he went on to say he had been thinking of other ways in which they might help on the good cause. The sick in the hospitals would want delicacies, currant jelly for one thing, so they would watch the ripening currants on their own bushes, pick them carefully when just right for use, buy sugar with their pocket money, and get mother to make the jelly, to teach them how to do it."

"You're right, Milly. They are children to be proud of," the doctor said, his tones a little unsteady, a telltale moisture in his eyes. "But had our boy anything else to suggest?"

"Yes. They could sell eggs and chickens and spend the money on comforts for the soldiers who are fighting so bravely for their country."

"'But we mustn't use our missionary hens' eggs and chickens for that,' Marcia said, and Percy replied quickly, 'Oh, no, only the others. We are not to sacrifice one good cause for another but must do all we can for both.'"

# CHAPTER X

WHEN RUPERT KEITH parted from parents and sisters to go to the aid of his imperiled country, both he and they had hope that the war would be at an end within the ninety days for which the call for troops was made. But before that time had expired, the hope had vanished, and both he and his brother Don had reenlisted "for three years, or the war."

Wallace Ormsby and his company had done likewise and were off to the seat of war, with Cyril Keith as chaplain of the regiment.

It was in Dr. Landreth's heart to go to the help of the sick and wounded—who, alas, were becoming very many—but he had yielded to the entreaties of his brothers-in-law that he would stay at home and care for their aged parents, their wives, and children, Cyril leaving his little family at his father's.

Most of the ladies of Pleasant Plains—conspicuous among them Mildred and her sisters—continued their labors almost unremittingly, and box after box of clothing and whatever else seemed likely to be of service to the men in the field or hospital was dispatched to those who were engaged in the work of distribution.

And Mildred's children were diligently, persever-
ingly carrying out their plans for the same object.

They did not know that their mother had
overheard the laying of them but were not long in
confiding them to her, for "mother" was to each
one the dearest, best, and most intimate friend.
They were open as the day with her, and scarcely
had, or desired to have, a thought or feeling con-
cealed from her.

Nor were the confidences expected to be all on
one side. The parents talked freely to their children
of family affairs, consulted their tastes and wishes
in many things, and made them feel a personal
interest in all that pertained to domestic economy
and comfort.

Mildred exacted prompt and implicit obedience
in their early infancy, and as they grew older,
found it no very difficult task to guide and govern
them by appealing to their reason and affection,
enforcing all her requirements by bringing forward the teachings of Scripture. A "thus saith the
Lord" was to her and to them the end of all con-
troversy, a final settlement of every doubt as to
what should be believed or done under any and all
circumstances.

Percy came to her one day with a question that
greatly surprised her.

"Mother, is it ever right, under any circumstances, to tell a falsehood?"

"My son!" she exclaimed. "How can you ask me
that? The Bible teaches that God is a God of truth,
that He hates lying. I think there is no sin that is
more frequently and strongly condemned in the
Scriptures, or against which more fearful threaten-
ings are recorded.

"'All liars shall have their part in the lake which burneth with fire and brimstone.' The Bible tells us that lying lips shall be put to silence; that the Lord hateth a lying tongue; that 'a lying tongue is but for a moment'; 'he that speaketh lies shall not escape'; 'he that speaketh lies shall perish'; that the Devil is a liar, and the father of it; and, in the description given us of the New Jerusalem, it is said, 'And there shall in no wise enter into it anything that defileth, neither whatsoever worketh abomination or maketh a lie.'

"But, Percy, you have been taught all this from your earliest years."

"Yes, mother, and I never thought it could possibly be anything else than very wicked to say what was not true—till today, when Stuart Ormsby and I were talking with some of the other boys about the war and what a fellow should do if the Rebs captured him and threatened his life if he didn't give them information that would help them to get an advantage over the Federals."

"And what were the opinions?" asked Mildred.

"Almost all thought he should answer in whatever way would be best for the Federal cause," replied Percy. "But I said I thought the only right thing would be to tell the truth—or say nothing, even if they should shoot or hang you for refusing to give them information.

"Then cousin Stuart astonished me very much by asserting that it was right to tell a lie when a good end was to be gained by it, that the Bible taught it, because Rahab the Harlot told a lie to save Joshua's spies form being taken by their enemies, and the Apostle Paul praises her for it in his Epistle to the Hebrews."

"Praises her for telling a lie?" exclaimed Mildred. "No, indeed! It is her faith, only her faith, that he commends."

"'By faith the harlot Rahab perished not with them that believed not, when she had received the spies with peace,' is what he says.

"Bring the Bible, turn to the second chapter of Joshua, and let us see her confession of faith."

Percy obeyed.

"This is what you refer to, I suppose, mother?" he said, then read aloud:

"'. . . for the Lord your God, he is God in heaven above, and in earth beneath.'"

"Yes, and it strikes me as a very strong confession of faith for one with Rahab's limited opportunities, and in concealing the spies, she showed her faith by her works. Joshua said, 'Rahab the harlot shall live, she and all that are with her in the house, because she hid the messengers that we sent.' Yet I cannot see that either he or the apostle uttered any commendation of her falsehood, and I am sure they could have meant none, because in the Epistle to the Romans, Paul distinctly and strongly repudiates the doctrine that it is right to do evil that good may come."

Taking the Bible from Percy's hand, she turned to the third chapter of Romans and read aloud:

"'But if our unrighteousness commend the righteousness of God, what shall we say? Is God unrighteous who taketh vengeance? (I speak as a man) God forbid: for then how shall God judge the world? For if the truth of God hath more abounded through my lie unto his glory; why yet am I also judged as a sinner? And not rather (as we be slanderously reported, and as some affirm that we say), Let us do evil, that good may come? whose damnation is just.'"

"'Whose damnation is just,'" repeated Percy musingly. "I don't see how He could well express a stronger condemnation, or how anybody, remembering what He says there, could for a moment suppose He meant to approve of a lie told from any motive whatever.

"Mother, you wouldn't tell a lie for anything, would you? Not even if it was to save your own life or that of some one you loved? Father, for instance."

"I can only say I ought not to, that I ought to do right and leave the result entirely with God," she answered. "But I cannot be sure till I am tried that I should have strength to do the right thing under so fearful a temptation to forsake it."

"But I am sure you would, mother dear," Percy said emphatically, "because you have such faith in God and in His promise, 'As thy days, so shall thy strength be.' But I'm not nearly so certain of myself," he went on. "And if the war should last till I'm old enough to go, I shall want you to pray a great deal for me, mother, that I may be strong to do the right thing under every trial and temptation and may never act the coward under any circumstances."

"But be a brave soldier, not of the government only but of Jesus Christ," she said, smiling on him through tears. "My boy, I would have you that now, I would have you enlist under Him this very hour, and then, should the time come when you will be called to serve your country on the field of battle, you will be ready, and I shall be able to part from you in the full assurance that we shall meet again in a better land, even if never more in this."

The other children had come in during the conversation and were quietly listening. There was a moment's silence broken by Stuart.

"Even such a boy as I might enlist in that army, mother?" he said half in assertion, half inquiringly.

"Yes," she answered. "Marcia too, and Fan. All who would gain the victory over sin and Satan and at last enter into that blessed land where all is holiness and life and peace, the glorious inheritance bought with the precious blood of Christ, must enlist in that army and fight the good fight of faith."

"What are we to fight, mother?" asked little Fan, leaning on her lap and gazing inquiringly up into her face. "I thought it was wicked to fight, 'cept the Rebs. That's what they call the bad, naughty folks my uncles have gone to fight, you know."

"We must fight our evil natures," her mother answered. "When we want to do or say something that we know to be wrong, we must fight hard with ourselves to keep from doing or saying it. And when we don't want to do what we know we ought, we must be very determined and do it."

"I don't b'lieve I like that kind of soldiering," returned Fan, shaking her curly head. "Indeed, I don't want to be any kind of a soldier."

"But the dear Lord Jesus is the captain of that army, and calls us to be soldiers under Him," her mother said, stroking the child's hair and looking down lovingly into her eyes. "Would my little Fan turn away from Him, the dear Saviour who died that she might live? The dear Saviour who loves her far better than father or mother does?"

"No. I'll be His little soldier if He'll take care of me and teach me how to fight," was the quick, earnest rejoinder. "Will He, mother?"

"Yes, my darling, if you ask Him with all your heart. He never turns any away who come to Him. 'Him that cometh unto me, I will in no wise cast out,' He says."

"But maybe I'm too little, mother."

"No, don't you remember how He said, 'Suffer the little children to come unto me, and forbid them not: for of such is the kingdom of God'?

"It is easier for children to come with their young, tender hearts than for older people whose hearts have grown hard with staying away so long from Jesus, and serving sin and Satan."

"Mother," said Percy, "there is another question we boys have been discussing: whether a man who dies fighting for his country is sure to go to heaven because he gives his life for her defense?

"Of course, I know very well that it is not so. Still, I should like to hear what you have to say about it."

"Do not rely too much on what I say, my boy," returned Mildred, "or on the opinion of any human creature.

"'To the law and to the testimony: if they speak not according to this word, it is because there is no light in them.'

"The Bible—God's own holy word—is the only infallible rule of faith and practice. And what are its teachings?

"'Believe on the Lord Jesus Christ, and thou shalt be saved.'

"'There is none other name under heaven given among men, whereby we must be saved.

"'By the deeds of the law there shall no flesh be justified in his sight.'

"Jesus said, 'Verily, verily, I say unto you, he

that entereth not by the door into the sheepfold, but climbeth up some other way, the same is a thief and a robber. . . . I am the door; by me if any man enter in, he shall be saved, and shall go in and out, and find pasture.'

"Patriotism is a good thing, and those who lay down their lives for their country are worthy to be held in loving remembrance, but nothing short of faith in Jesus Christ can secure the soul's salvation. Ah, would that all our soldiers had it!"

"They would make all the better soldiers for it, wouldn't they, mother?" Percy said.

"Yes, history proves it. Cromwell's Ironsides, sternly religious men, were almost invincible. The Waldeneses made excellent soldiers, even when fighting the battles of princes who had persecuted them and their forefathers but to whom they owed political allegiance.

"And bravery and fidelity are the natural result of being at peace with God and earnestly desirous to honor Him."

"Mother," Marcia said with a look of surprise and perplexity, "I thought all the men that are fighting for the Union were good men and all the ones that fight against it were very bad men."

"No, dear, there are good men and bad in both armies. Few people are altogether bad, and some who do love God and try to keep his commandments still love their country well enough to fight to save her from being torn to pieces.

"Then some good men on the other side have been deceived and made to believe falsehoods in regard to the government and the people of the North, and so are fighting against the right, believing it to be the wrong."

At that moment a rather heavy, determined step came through kitchen and dining room, then a portly figure filled the open doorway of the sitting room where mother and children were.

It was that of our old acquaintance Celestia Ann, who still reigned in Mrs. Keith's kitchen and was a privileged character in the entire connection.

"Good evenin', Mis' Mildred," she said (she never addressed any daughter of the family by her married name). "You're all well, I s'pose?"

"Yes," Mildred answered, "quite well, thank you, Celestia Ann. How are you? I was not expecting to see you, for they told me at father's that you had gone home for a few days. Sit down and tell me how you found them all there."

"Yes, I did go, but you see I've come back," replied Celestia Ann, accepting the invitation to be seated. "I just went to say goodbye to my two nephews, brother Joe's boys. They've 'listed as privateers and are off to the war.

"They call this a civil war, Mis' Mildred, but I'm bound to say I don't see nothin' civil about it—so fur anyhow.

"Now that shootin' down of that nice young Colonel Ellsworth just for haulin' down their pesky old Confederate flag—do you call that civil? Of course, he was doin' his dooty, fer the Stars and Stripes was the only flag that had a right to be wavin' there.

"And was it civil for the Rebs to steal United States property, or to fire on the troops that was mindin' the President's call fer 'em to come to Washington?"

"No, Celestia Ann, I should say it was putting it very mildly to call that very uncivil," laughed Percy.

"Well," she went on, "that wasn't all I come in fer—just to free my mind about the uncivilness that's goin' on—but I see you've got lots of currants in your garden, and they're just ripe enough to make prime jelly."

"Yes," cried the children in eager chorus, "we've been saving them up for the poor sick and wounded soldiers in the hospitals, and mother is going to make the jelly for us."

"You'd better let me do it, Mis' Mildred," said Celestia Ann. "You know I'm a master hand at the business and a heap stronger than you, and I am fairly spoiling to do something to help the good cause."

"Thank you," returned Mildred. "I accept your kind offer gladly, as it will give me more time to work on these shirts. But you have already done a great deal, Celestia Ann. You seem always to have a soldier's stocking growing in your hands when done with your housework and cooking. I wonder how many pairs you have knitted?"

"'Bout a half-dozen, I guess. But that ain't nothin', so I want to make that jelly. And I've a spare hour or so now, and I'll help the children to pick 'em. Get your buckets and baskets, and come along young-uns, if your mother's willin'."

The offer was gladly accepted. Mildred and the children expressing not only willingness to follow Celestia Ann's lead but gratitude for her proffered assistance.

In a few moments they were all busily at work among the currant bushes.

107

# CHAPTER XI

IT WAS A hot July evening, hardly a breath of air stirring, and the group of adults and children gathered on the wide porch at Mr. Keith's seemed strangely depressed.

He, the patriarch of the family, was among them, sitting in an attitude of deep despondency, his gray head bowed on his breast, his hands lying listlessly on the arms of his easy chair.

His faithful wife sat close at his side, her face pale and sad yet quite calm and resigned.

Their daughters Mildred, Zillah, Annis, and Cyril's wife were there with all their children, and Dr. Landreth was pacing up and down the path leading from the porch to the gate with an air of disturbance most unusual with him.

The prattle of the little ones was almost the only sound that had been heard for some moments when Percy broke the silence with a sudden exclamation:

"I don't know how to stand it! I just wish I was old enough to go! Father, what do you think the government will do? They won't give it up, surely?"

"Certainly not," said the doctor. "This disaster will but rouse the loyal North to a fiercer determination and greater effort to suppress the rebellion.

"And the right must triumph in the end. I cannot believe that this grand republic will be allowed to go to pieces, this star of hope to the oppressed of all nations to go out in darkness."

"No," said Mr. Keith, lifting his head. "But we have sinned greatly as a nation—we have oppressed both the Indian and the Negro, and national sins are punished in this world; therefore, I fear this is to be a long and bloody war."

"Yes," responded his wife, "yet we may take comfort in the thought that God reigns, that He is slow to anger, and of great mercy, and will never leave or forsake those who put their trust in Him."

"And," she added with an effort, "there is certainly a possibility that this report of Rupert being among the wounded is a false one."

"Yes, mother," said Mildred. "And we know that he is a Christian and that in whatever place or condition he may be tonight, he has with him One who loves him far better than we do and is perfectly able to give him both ease of body and peace of mind."

"And will not allow him or any of His children to suffer one unneeded pang," added her mother.

"Oh, for a stronger faith! A faith that would enable us just to lie still in His hands and never doubt that He will cause all things to work together for our good!"

"And for the good of this land, and the best interests of Zion," added the doctor. "Yet it is impossible not to feel a terrible heartache over this defeat."

At that moment, Celestia Ann came hurrying round the corner of the house.

"Doctor!" she cried excitedly. "Where's this Bull Run they talk about, where they say there's been a big battle?"

"In Virginia," he answered.

"That's a long ways off, isn't it?" she queried.

"Yes, farther off than Washington."

"Well, now, I'd like to know if them nephews of mine that 'listed as privateers t'other day, was in the fight?"

"That I can't tell you," he said.

"Isn't there a list o' names in the papers?" she demanded.

"A list of killed and wounded—probably not a full one—but by no means of all who were in the engagement. Here is a paper that gives quite a full account," he added, taking one from this pocket and handing it to her.

"Thank you. I'll fetch it back when I've read it," she said, disappearing in the direction of the kitchen.

The weather was so warm, the painful excitement so great, that few people in the town retired early that night. Mildred lingered at her father's, keeping her children with her, till she could persuade him and her mother to seek their couch, and try to get some sleep.

"Mother, I'm so tired and sleepy," fretted little Fan as they passed in at their own gate.

"Yes, dear, I know you are, and you shall go at once to your nice bed," was the kindly rejoinder.

"I'm ready for mine, too," said Stuart.

"It's very warm to go into the house," said Marcia. "Mother, mayn't Percy and I sit here in the porch a little while?"

"Yes, if you both wish it. I'll be down again presently and join you."

"I hope father won't have to go to the country tonight," sighed the little girl when left alone with her older brother.

"He has gone," said Percy, "and he told me he hardly hoped to get home before morning. But why are you particularly concerned about it tonight?"

"Oh, because I feel afraid. Such dreadful things are going on, and I read in the papers that the Rebels threaten to bring the war up North and burn our cities. And maybe they'll come here and burn us out and take everything we have. Kill us, too."

"I don't think they can," said Percy. "It's easy to boast but not always quite so easy to act. I don't believe they'll succeed in getting into Washington even, much less come all the way up here."

"Maybe not. I hope not, I'm sure. But there are bad men—burglars and murderers—everywhere almost. And now so many of the best men have gone to the war from this town—uncle Wallace and ever so many more from the families right round here—and when father's gone to the country, there's hardly a man near us except grandpa, who is so old and feeble."

"Well, sis, try not to be afraid, and I'll do my best to protect you," said Percy, putting his arm round her as she sat by his side.

"I know you will, for you are a good, kind brother," she said. "But you are not strong enough to fight a man, and more than one might come."

"'It is better to trust in the Lord than to put confidence in man,'" quoted her mother, returning in time to hear her last sentence.

She sat down as she spoke, and in a moment Marcia's head was in her lap.

"What is it that troubles my little daughter?" Mildred said. "We need not tremble or be afraid, for we have a better protector than even your dear father."

"'The fear of man bringeth a snare: but whoso putteth his trust in the Lord shall be safe.'"

"Mother," said Percy, "what a good text that would be for one who was tempted to tell a lie to save his life. You remember the talk we had about that not very long ago?"

"Yes, I do," she replied. "And that would be an instance in which the fear of man would bring a snare, a temptation to disobey a plain command of God. Yet it is impossible for anyone to be in such extremity that God could not deliver him. And, oh, what rest and peace is wrought by an abiding, unwavering trust in Him!

"'Whoso hearkeneth unto me shall dwell safely, and shall be quiet from fear of evil.'"

"Does that mean bad men that might come to rob and murder us, mother?" asked Marcia, in half-tremulous tones.

"Yes, dear. With the might God for our Rock and Refuge and Defense, we need fear neither the designs of evil men nor danger in any other form."

"But we must fear God, mother, mustn't we?"

"Yes, dear, not with a slavish, guilty fear (we need have none of that if we come to Jesus and have all our sins forgiven for His dear sake) but with a holy, filial affection that will lead us to keep His commandments, not finding them grievous. We are to be followers of God as dear children. I think you can understand it pretty well by the feeling you have for your father and mother."

"Yes, ma'am! Oh, yes!"

Mildred went on. "Our life in this world is like a journey over a narrow road beset on each side with snares and pitfalls. And the only way to travel it safely is to take heed to our steps and keep close to

Him who is the Guard and Guide of all who put their trust in Him.

"While we do that, we have no occasion to fear. Indeed, to fear danger when God has promised to take care of us is a sin. It is doubting His word, and the Bible says:

"'He that believeth not God, hath made him a liar.' And it mentions the fearful and the unbelieving among the liars and murderers and other wicked ones who shall have their part in the lake which burneth with fire and brimstone.

"People may make themselves exceedingly unhappy—and I think many do—by indulging in doubts and fears. They are all the time concerned lest some accident happen to their dear ones or themselves; lest they lose health, property, reputation, friends; lest some calamity befall them. They cannot enjoy the present because of forebodings of evil in store for their future."

"They must be very miserable," remarked Percy.

"Yes, and I hope my dear children will not be of their number."

"No, I hope not. But troubles and trials do come to everybody, mother."

"They do, but they are not half so hard to bear when received in a spirit of cheerful submission, as needed discipline from a loving Father's hands. And trials and afflictions, when regarded in that light, are not anticipated with fear and dread.

"My darlings, the only way to be happy is to trust God in everything and be content with His will.

"He is always near us, His ear always open to our cries, His heart full of love to His children, His power to succor and to save infinite.

"'He doeth according to his will in the army of heaven, and among the inhabitants of the earth; and none can stay his hand, or say unto him, What doest thou?'"

"Mother," Percy said, half in assertion, half inquiringly, "you can't help being sad and anxious about the country and for my uncles, especially poor uncle Rupert?"

"No," she sighed, "my faith is not so strong as it should be, yet it is strong enough to give me great peace in staying my heart on the God of Israel. I know He rules and reigns and will do what is best for both my dear country and my beloved brothers."

"Mother, I don't feel so afraid as I did," said Marcia, "but won't you say some more of those Bible verses that teach us not to fear?"

"The Bible is full of them," Mildred said. "They are so many and so sweet, it is difficult to choose among them.

"'I will say of the Lord, He is my refuge and my fortress: my God; in him will I trust. . . . Because thou hast made the Lord, which is my refuge, even the most High, thy habitation; there shall no evil befall thee, neither shall any plague come nigh thy dwelling.'

"'He that keepeth thee will not slumber. Behold, he that keepeth Israel shall neither slumber nor sleep. . . . The Lord shall preserve thee from all evil: he shall preserve thy soul. The Lord shall preserve thy going out, and thy coming in, from this time forth, and even for evermore.'

"What is there for us to fear, my little Mar, if we quite believe all those sweet words?"

"Nothing, mother. Oh, I'm glad they are in the Bible! And thank you for repeating them to me.

How I pity those who have no sweet Bible words to comfort them and help them not to be afraid!"

"Yes, poor creatures! We must do all we can to send them Bibles and missionaries."

"But it is growing very late. Percy, my son, you may help me to shut up the house, and we will go to bed."

He rose with alacrity. "Let me do it all, mother, if you are not afraid to trust me."

Mildred's brain was so active, thought for her country and dear absent brothers so busy in it, that she lay a long while awake, but at length she slept.

It seemed to her that it had not been very long, that she'd scarcely more than lost herself for a moment, when a knock at the outer kitchen door aroused her.

She sprang from her bed, ran to a back window, drew aside the curtain, and leaning out, asked, "Who is there? Someone wanting the doctor?"

"It's on'y me, mistis," answered a trembling voice, "on'y me an' Jim. An' we's mos' dead wid trablin' and wid starvin'."

"Rachel!" exclaimed Mildred in half-breathless astonishment. "I'll let you in in one minute."

Waiting only to throw on a dressing gown, she hurried down and opened the door.

Rachel stumbled in and dropped, half fainting, into a chair, Jim stepping wearily in after her.

It was too dark to see their faces, but Mildred could hear their labored breathing.

"Sit down, Jim," she said. "Don't think you must stand, out of respect to me, when you are just ready to drop."

She struck a match and lighted a lamp as she spoke.

"Oh, my poor Rachel!" she cried as the light flashed on the woman's face. "You do look half dead! But I hope food and rest may be all you need, and you shall have them at once."

She hastened to bring milk, bread, butter, and meat and set them before the evidently half-famished creatures, refusing to hear a word of their story till they had eaten and drunk to the satisfying of their appetites.

By that time, the doctor had returned, and together they listened to what the fugitives had to tell. It was a brief account, enlarged upon the next day after a long sleep had still further restored their almost exhausted energies.

"How is it that you have only Jim with you, Rachel?" was the doctor's first question.

"'Cuz he's all I'se got lef', Marse Charlie." And Rachel's eyes filled, and her bosom heaved with sobs. "De baby she cotched a dreful cold on de way back to de house ob bondage, w'en Marse Cass carry us back, an' she's die 'mos' soon as we's got dar. Den Sam, my po' ole man, he's sole down Souf, an' I'se neber see him no mo'. Jim an' me, we's lef' behin', an' we's bofe wukin', wukin' fer Marse Cass an' de mistis.

"We's often talkin' 'bout runnin' off ag'in w'en we gits de chance, but dat doan' come till mistis she gwine die, an' Marse Cass he's off to de wah.

"Den dar's de news dat de Yanks is cumin'. An' Jim an' me we's not 'fraid de Yanks, but de res' am, an' eberbody's gwine be dat busy lookin' out fer de Yanks, dey woan' hab' no time to be settin' de bloodhoun's on our track or chasin' after we uns wid dere guns and shootin' us down. Den Jim he say, 'Mammy, de time's come; let's be off fer Marse

116

Charlie's.' An' we done start dat bery night, trablin' towa'ds de norf star."

"And a long, weary journey you've had of it," remarked the doctor compassionately.

"But I think you will be permitted to stay this time."

"Does yo', Marse Charlie?" she asked eagerly. "Bress de good Lawd, ef dat's so. Who yo' t'inks gwine beat in dis wah?"

"The government, Rachel. The government will surely succeed in the end, though there may have to be a great deal of terrible fighting first.

"And I think we may hope to have no further trouble with the Fugitive Slave Law that sent you back to what you call the 'house of bondage.'"

"Dat's de bes' news, Marse Charlie!" she said, tears of joy rolling down her cheeks.

"I'se mos' pow'ful glad to git hyar again, but my heart's cl'ar broke 'bout my po' ole man, Sam."

"Cheer up, Rachel. Perhaps he may be able to follow you one of these days," returned the doctor, speaking more hopefully than he felt.

"But it is very late—or rather early, long past midnight—and you are quite worn out. You must rest now for some hours.

"Your old home is still vacant, your furniture still there, and you may take possession at once if you will."

He handed her the key as he spoke, adding, "It is not in need of airing; the doors and windows were open nearly all day."

She poured out her thanks. "You's mighty good to we uns, Marse Charlie, an' me an' Jim's mor'n obliged."

Then, taking a lantern Mildred had lighted for

her, she asked to be called when it was time to get breakfast, saying she feared she would oversleep.

"No, I shall not call you," replied Mildred. "You are to sleep as long as you can and are not to begin work till you are able to do it."

"Mistis, you's de kin'est lady in de land, and I'se willin' for to work my fingers to de bone for you an' Marse Charlie an' yo' chill'n," returned the grateful woman, dropping a curtsy. Then, with a good night to each, she strode away in the direction of her former home, Jim following at her heels.

"Poor things! They look half dead with fatigue," remarked Mildred as her husband closed and locked the door after them. "But what a pleasant surprise the children will have in the morning!"

"Yes," returned the doctor. "And I hope to see my good wife leading an easier life when Rachel has had time to rest and recover her strength.

"I am very glad they are here but sorry they arrived at night and robbed you of your sleep."

"I hope to get over that in a day or two," she said, smiling up at him as he led the way to their room. "But I think the heat and troubled thought stole more of my ability to sleep than their coming did."

"Ah, yes," he sighed. "The heat has been very oppressive, and the news from the seat of war such as must give a heartache to every lover of this land.

"But, dear wife," he added, setting down the lamp he had been carrying and taking her in his arms for a moment, "let us try to leave ourselves, our loved ones, and our country all in the hands of Him who doeth all things well."

"Yes," she said, laying her head on his shoulder while her tears fell fast, "I am trying to do so, and with some measure of success, but the image of my poor wounded, perhaps dying brother is continually with me, and I am longing to fly to his assistance."

"I hope we shall have better news tomorrow," he said tenderly, "or rather today, for, see, the day is already breaking. So get to bed, dearest, and sleep as long as you can. Don't feel that there is any necessity for rising at your usual early hour."

"If you will do the same," she said, "for I am sure you need rest and sleep quite as much as I do."

The children woke at their usual early hour but, finding that their parents still slept, were careful to make no noise to awaken them.

Mildred had trained her boys and girls to thoughtfulness for their father, who was often sleeping off the fatigue of a night of anxiety and unrest at the very time when they rose refreshed and invigorated from their slumbers.

Their bedrooms adjoined hers, and the little girl's room had a door of communication with it.

On waking, Marcia stepped quietly to this door and peeped in. A smile of satisfaction overspread her face. She turned with a warning gesture toward Fan, then stole softly in and closed the blinds, lest the bright sunlight should awaken the beloved sleepers.

"We must dress and go down very quietly, Fan dear," she whispered when she came back. "Father and mother are both asleep, and I know they wouldn't be if they didn't need rest and sleep."

Fan nodded assent, and presently they left the room and went softly down to the kitchen, where they found Percy and Stuart standing gazing about them in wonder and astonishment.

It was an unheard of thing in their experience for the kitchen, or indeed any room in the house, to be left in disorder overnight, but Mildred had been too weary and preoccupied to clear away the remains of the repast spread for Rachel and Jim.

Marcia was the first to break the amazed silence that had fallen upon them. "Somebody's been in the house!" she exclaimed in a tone of affright. "More than one person, for there are two plates! Oh, I hope nothing's stolen!"

"Father and mother!" gasped Stuart. "Mother's 'most always down before this!"

"They're in bed, fast asleep," said Marcia.

"Oh, that is good!" cried both the boys.

"If thieves have been in, they didn't go upstairs, I think," said Percy. "But we'll look round the rooms and see if anything has been taken."

They all went together through dining and sitting rooms, parlor and office, but without discovering that anything was missing.

"I'll tell you what I think," said Percy as they reentered the kitchen. "Father must have come home hungry and brought somebody with him."

"Why, yes, that's it, of course!" said Stuart in a tone of relief. "We might have thought of that at first. Percy, I'll make the fire and put on the kettle while you feed and water the horses and cow. Can't we children get up a nice breakfast and have it ready by the time mother comes down?"

"Yes, if she'll only be good enough to sleep half an hour longer," said Marcia.

"Fan can set the table, and you can go out to the garden and gather some radishes and tomatoes while I make some of those delicate rolls father is so fond of."

"Yes," returned Stuart, "and I'll grind the coffee and get some fresh eggs."

Percy was already at the lower end of the lot on his way to the stable. Passing the window of the little frame house, he happened to glance in, and a sight greeted his eyes that gave him a greater shock of surprise than that other in the kitchen.

He stood for a moment gazing in breathless astonishment, then turned and rushed back.

"Stuart!" he cried, meeting his brother coming down the garden path with a basket in his hand. "What do you think?"

"Oh, have you found the thieves?" was Stuart's answering exclamation.

"Thieves? No, it's Rachel and Jim!"

Pointing over his shoulder, he added, "They're lying in there, both of them fast asleep."

"Oh, are they?" cried Stuart joyfully. "Oh, aren't you glad! Now I think we know who was eating in the kitchen last night. Dear me! I'd like to speak to them and say how glad I am they've come back. But I wonder Rachel doesn't come and get breakfast."

"You forget how tired they must be," said Percy. "And neither mother nor any of the rest of us would want them to go to work before they had had time to rest."

"Of course not, so we won't disturb them. But let's run and tell the girls. The news is too good to keep."

Marcia, busy gathering together the materials for making the rolls, stood still in astonishment as her two brothers came rushing in with faces full of excitement.

"What's the matter?" she asked. "But you don't look as if it was anything dreadful."

"No, it isn't," they cried. "Rachel and Jim are asleep yonder in their old home."

They were quite satisfied with the surprise and delight she showed.

Fan, too, seemed much pleased, though she was scarcely able to remember the returned fugitives. But she had often heard them spoken of and knew that their coming meant help for "mother," which was quite enough to fill her heart with gladness.

But work must not be neglected at this hour in the morning, and in another minute the boys were speeding away down the garden path again, and Marcia had turned her attention to the preparation of her rolls.

Breakfast was just ready to set on the table when the doctor and Mildred came downstairs.

A very inviting meal it was, too, and words of commendation that made them very happy were generously meted out to the children.

As they were leaving the table, Rachel made her appearance, uttering many apologies for over-sleeping and for her travel-stained condition.

She was kindly assured that none were needed and that she would not be allowed to do much that day but rest and eat.

# CHAPTER XII

IN A FEW DAYS the anxiety of Rupert Keith's relatives was somewhat relieved by the news that he was seriously, though not dangerously, wounded and that his wife was with him in the hospital to which he had been conveyed.

In the meantime, Rachel had recovered from her fatigue and was proving herself as efficient as formerly. She rejoiced greatly in her restoration to her home with "Marse Charlie and his wife and chill'n," but she mourned the loss of her "ole man" and was very anxious and troubled in regard to his welfare.

The months rolled on, the struggle between loyalty and rebellion still continuing, victory perching now upon the one banner and now upon the other, and some of the baser sort in the North beginning to cry out in favor of abandoning the cause of the Union. And that was not all, for some also were doing what they dared to give aid and comfort to the enemy.

Summer had passed, autumn, too, and winter, when one April day there came news of a terrible battle in progress on the banks of the Tennessee. The first tidings were of defeat, and, oh, the sorrow and anxiety in Pleasant Plains! For many of her best and bravest, including Wallace Ormsby and Cyril Keith, were in the army engaged.

Zillah was, of course, even more distressed than the rest of the family, fearing that she was already a widow or that her husband was lying wounded and suffering on the bloody field of battle.

Soon after hearing the news, she ran over to Dr. Landreth's to pour out into Mildred's sympathizing ear the fears, griefs, and anxieties that had come upon her like an overwhelming flood.

Mildred did her best to cheer and comfort, and with her heart bleeding for her country and anxious fears for her brother and brother-in-law assailing her, it was no difficult task to sympathize.

"My poor sister," she said, folding Zillah in her arms, "I can imagine how you feel, thinking how distressed I should be if Charlie were in Wallace's place.

"And we must all be anxious for Cyril, though he is, of course, in much less danger than Wallace.

"But let us stay our hearts on God, who will never leave or forsake either them or us.

"We must try to keep this news from mother as long as possible."

"Yes, that was why I came first to you. Oh, I wish dear mother could be spared all the sorrow and anxiety brought by this dreadful war! But it cannot be, for she—like all the rest of us—is eager every day to see the papers, wanting to know all that can be learned from them. We can't help wanting to hear every report, though so often what is told one day is contradicted the next."

"Yes, that is very true, sister," said Mildred. "And perhaps tomorrow the reported defeat of today may be turned into a victory."

"Yes, or, as the fighting seems to be still going on, perhaps the bravery and persistence of our troops may turn it into a victory, with the help of God," she added. "And, Milly, I for one shall be praying for it every moment of this day."

"Yes," said Mildred. "What a blessing that we may—we women who can do neither the fighting nor the nursing of the sick and wounded—help in that way, as well as in providing hospital stores and clothing for our brave boys in blue."

The sisters were alone in the sitting room, both at work, knitting soldiers' stockings while they talked. Zillah had brought one in her hands, though stopping now and then to brush away a tear. But presently the doorbell rang, and Rachel ushered in a neighbor who was by no means so loyal as themselves.

Knowing that, they were not delighted to see her but gave her a pleasant "Good morning," and Mildred, drawing forward a comfortable chair, invited her to be seated, wondering within herself all the while what could have brought Mrs. Boyle to call upon her on this particular morning, they having barely a speaking acquaintance.

She was not kept long in suspense, for the visitor announced her errand as soon as seated.

"Mrs. Landreth," she said, "I came to ask if you will lend me a pattern of the apron your youngest little girl has on this morning. I noticed it as the children passed my house on their way to school."

"Certainly," replied Mildred. "I have it here in my work basket." And as she spoke, she picked up a little roll of paper and handed it to her caller.

"Thank you. I'll send it home when I've cut one off it," said Mrs. Boyle.

"It's awful bad news the papers bring us this morning, Mrs. Ormsby." Zillah bowed in silence.

"Don't you begin to regret now that you encouraged your husband to go?"

"No," returned Zillah emphatically, "not in the very least! I could not then—and I would not now—withhold my best and dearest from my country in her hour of need. And I am proud of my husband's readiness to give himself to such a noble cause!"

"But if he should never come back?"

"Then I shall feel that it is far better to be even the widow of a brave, patriotic soldier than the wife of a traitor or poltroon," returned Zillah, flashing a scornful look at her interlocutor.

The woman flushed angrily. "I don't believe in this war!" she said. "I didn't believe in it in the first place, and now that there's been so much bloodshed, I think it's high time a stop was put to it."

"Unconditional surrender on the part of those who are so wickedly rebelling against the best government in the world would put a stop to it at once," retorted Zillah.

"They ought to have been let go in peace," remarked her antagonist.

"They didn't even ask permission to go," said Zillah. "They walked out without so much as saying 'by your leave,' and then turned round and began to fight the government which they had already robbed of arms and ammunition to use in assailing her."

"They had their grievances, same as our Revolutionary fathers."

"Grievances, indeed!" cried Zillah indignantly. "I should like to know what they were?"

"Mrs. Boyle," said Mildred, opening a table drawer and taking a folded newspaper from it, "I have here a speech delivered last summer in Louisville by the Hon. Joseph Holt of Kentucky, and I should like to answer your objections to the defense of our country against this armed rebellion by reading you some extracts from it.

"You have just asserted that the traitors had their grievances like our Revolutionary fathers, who had borne with many and great wrongs, much of intolerable oppression, before they took up arms to secure freedom for themselves and us.

"But Mr. Holt says (and truly), 'The rights of no state have been invaded, no man's property has been despoiled, no man's liberty abridged, no man's life oppressively jeopardized by the action of the government. Under its benign indulgence, rills of public and private property have swelled into rivulets, and from rivulets into rivers every brimming in their fullness. And everywhere, and at all periods of its history, its ministrations have fallen as gently on the people of the United States as do the dews of a summer's night on the flowers and grass of the gardens and fields.'"

"Then what are they fighting for?" sniffed Mrs. Boyle.

"What to be sure!" said Mildred.

"Mr. Holt goes on to show that it is from the lust of power on the part of the leaders, and we know that where they have succeeded in inducing the people to forsake the Union and fight against the old flag, it has been by means of persistent falsehood in regard to the feeling at the North and the character of its people, calling them cowards, poltroons, Negro-worshippers, and asserting that one Southerner would prove equal, in a fight, to five Northerners; that there was no danger of a war; if the South would but stand up for its rights, the North would back down."

"Well, let them go, I say," repeated Mrs. Boyle.

"Listen," said Mildred, and she again read aloud.

"'If this rebellion succeeds, it will involve necessarily the destruction of our nationality, the division of our territory, the permanent disruption of the republic. It must rapidly dry up the sources of our material prosperity, and year by year we shall grow more impoverished, more and more revolutionary, enfeebled, and debased. Each returning election will bring with it ground for new civil commotions, and traitors, prepared to strike at the country that has rejected their claims to power, will spring up on every side. Disunion, once begun, will go on indefinitely. And under the influence of the fatal doctrine of secession, not only will state secede from states, but counties will secede from states also, and towns and cities from counties, until universal anarchy will be consummated in each individual who can make good his position by force of arms, claiming the right to defy the power of the government. Thus, we should have brought back to us the days of the robber barons with their moated castles and marauding retainers.'"

"But thousands of men are being killed in these battles," said Mrs. Boyle. "Thousands more are losing their limbs or getting terrible wounds that'll make them sufferers as long as they live. And thousands of widows and orphans will be left to poverty and distress. I think it's just awful."

"I entirely agree with you," returned Mildred. "And those whose unbridled ambition started these flames of war will have a dreadful account to render on the day of judgment. But they alone are responsible for it. As Mr. Holt truly says:

"'The arbitrament of the sword has been defiantly thrust into the face of the government, and there is no honorable escape from it. All guaranties and all attempts at adjustment by amendment to the Constitution are now scornfully rejected, and the leaders of the rebellion openly proclaim that they are fighting for their independence.'"

"Yes," said Mrs. Boyle, "that's it. And I say they've the same right to do that as the folks that lived here in America in the time of the Revolution."

"Wait," said Mildred, and again she read from the paper in her hand:

"'They are fighting for their independence! Independence of what? Independence of those laws which they themselves have aided in enacting; independence of that Constitution which their fathers framed, and to which they are parties and subjects by inheritance; independence of that beneficent government on whose treasury and honors they have grown strong and illustrious.

"'When a man commits a robbery on the highway, or a murder in the dark, he thereby declares his independence of the laws under which he lives and of the society of which he is a member. Should he, when arraigned, avow and justify the offense, he thereby becomes the advocate of the independence which he has thus declared. And if he resists, by force of arms, the officer, when dragging him to the prison, the penitentiary, or the gallows, he is thereby fighting for the independence he has thus declared and advocated. And such is the condition of the conspirators of the South at this moment.

"'It is no longer a question of Southern rights, which have never been violated, nor of the security of Southern institutions, which we know perfectly well have never been interfered with by the general government, but it is purely, with us, a question of national existence. In meeting this terrible issue which rebellion has made up with the loyal men of the country, we stand upon ground infinitely above all party lines and party platforms, ground as sublime as that on which our fathers stood when they fought the battles of the Revolution.'"

"Who is this Holt that knows so much?" demanded Mrs. Boyle as Mildred paused in the reading and turned to her with a look that seemed to ask, "Is not all this quite convincing?"

"Why, do you not know?" exclaimed Zillah. "He has been postmaster general, commissioner of patents, and secretary of war,† that last for a short time under Buchanan's administration."

"Well, the Confederates haven't marched their armies up here and destroyed our property."

"Not for want of the will to do so," said Zillah. "They did not hesitate to announce their purpose to burn and destroy Washington, Philadelphia, New York, and Boston, and had not the government raised an army to prevent their incursion into the North, they would, no doubt, have carried out their design."

"Let me read you one more paragraph, the closing one of this speech," said Mildred. "It seems to me so thoroughly convincing of the necessity for this war, so far as the government is concerned.

"'The principle on which this rebellion proceeds—that laws have in themselves no sanctions, no binding force upon the conscience, and that every man, under the promptings of interest or passion or caprice, may at will, and honorably too, strike at the government that shelters him—is one of utter demoralization and should be trodden out, as you would tread out a spark that has fallen on the roof of your dwelling. Its unchecked prevalence would resolve society into chaos and leave you without the slightest guaranty for life, liberty, or property. It is time that, in their majesty, the people of the United States should make known to the world that this government, in its dignity and power, is something worse than a moot court, and that the citizen who makes war upon it is a traitor, not only in theory, but in fact, and should have meted out to him a traitor's doom. The country wants no bloody sacrifices, but it must and will have peace, cost what it may.'"

Mrs. Boyle, hardly waiting for the conclusion, rose and, with a hasty "Good morning," beat a precipitate retreat.

"It is well for her that the Unionists of the North are so much less intolerant than the secessionists of the South," remarked Zillah. "But I do despise those who stay in the North, under the protection of the government, while at the same time they give all aid, sympathy, and comfort they can to its enemies. If they want to help the Rebels, let them go down there and share their privations and risks. We would be far better off without them."

"Yes," sighed Mildred, "the government has much more to contend with than the traitors at the South. There are traitors at the North also to watch and keep in check, men who are actually ready to fire our cities, poison their water supplies, liberate the prisoners of war, blow up steamers—not caring how many innocent lives they may sacrifice—spread disease by importing infected clothing, and there is the Copperhead press always ready to magnify Rebel successes and belittle ours."

"And even the loyal ones doing great mischief by publishing beforehand the plans of our generals and so, frequently defeating them, with the aid of the Northern traitors who contrive to transmit the information thus gained to the Rebel leaders," said Zillah. "It's just dreadful and wouldn't be allowed in any other country! 'Twould be far better for us all to go without the news we are so eager for."

Mildred arose. "Mother's coming," she said, hurrying out to meet her and Annis, who was with her.

They were mounting the steps of the porch as Mildred opened the front door.

One glance at their mother's face told her that she had heard the news: It was calm and sweet as was its wont, but it was very pale and sad.

"Zillah is here?" she asked in tones that trembled with emotion in spite of herself.

"My poor, dear child! She must be sadly anxious!"

"Yes, mother, she is here, and anxious, of course, but bearing it wonderfully well. We hoped the bad news had not reached you yet," Mildred said, leading the way into the sitting room.

In a moment, Zillah and her mother were clasped in each other's arms, both weeping.

"Dear, dear child!" Mrs. Keith murmured at length, softly smoothing her daughter's hair as if she were again indeed a child. "We will try to hope for the best for both our loved ones and our dear, imperilled country. Oh, these are times to try our souls! And there is no rest, no peace, but in staying our hearts in the God of Israel and firmly believing that nothing can happen unless permitted by Him, and that He doeth all things well.

"'The Lord liveth; and blessed be my rock; and let the God of my salvation be exalted.'"

"It is a comfort to know that Cyril is in less danger than Wallace and will be there to aid and comfort my dear husband if he is wounded or sick," said Zillah.

"Yes. Lucy made that remark herself this morning," said Annis, speaking of Cyril's wife.

"Sit down, mother dear, and rest," said Mildred, drawing forward an easy chair.

"I will sit down," Mrs. Keith answered, "but it is work I want—something to do for our poor soldiers—not rest. I have always found useful employment the best panacea for mental distress, when used in connection with faith in God and a determined casting of all care on Him."

"Then work you shall have, mother," Mildred said cheerfully. "Here are some soldiers' shirts that I cut out yesterday, and if you please, you may baste them for the machine."

"Give me one, Milly," requested Zillah.

"And let me run the machine while you cut out some more," said Annis. "Ah, mother dear, you know you have a bit of good news this morning that these sisters of mine will be glad to hear."

"Yes," Mrs. Keith said, "strange that I should have forgotten it. I have a letter from Aunt Wealthy, accepting my invitation to come to us for the summer and as much longer as she may like to stay.

"She says she is glad to come, now that she knows she can work here for the soldiers as well as in Lansdale. She loves us all and is lonely in her own home without Harry. He enlisted for the war, and there seems less and less hope of his speedy return."

"That is good news, indeed!" exclaimed both Mildred and Zillah. "When may we expect her?"

"She hopes to be with us early next month," replied their mother.

# CHAPTER XIII

THE NEXT DAY'S news was of victory to the Federal arms at Pittsburg Landing, the defeat and retreat of the Confederates.

These were joyful tidings to our friends in Pleasant Plains, as to all loyal Americans, but left them still in anxiety and suspense in regard to Cyril and Wallace.

At length, however, letters came from both, describing the battle, each from his own standpoint, and saying they had escaped its dangers and were entirely unharmed.

Wallace's letter contained other information, which sent Zillah in haste to her sisters's home.

"I have a letter from my husband," she announced joyously, "and a part of it will make Rachel's heart glad, or I am greatly mistaken. Where is she?"

Mildred stepped to the kitchen door and summoned her.

Rachel came with a half-frightened look on her pale face, but it fled at sight of the cheerful countenances of the ladies.

She glanced inquiringly from one to the other.

"I have some news for you, Rachel," said Zillah. "Your husband and mine are together. Listen, this is what Ormsby says." And she read aloud from the open letter in her hand:

"'It is not an unusual thing for the contrabands to come into our camp and ask to be allowed to stay in any capacity in which they can be made useful. Some days ago, as I was stepping out of my tent, I was accosted by a more than ordinarily agreeable-looking one.

"'"Marse Cap'n doan' yo' want a sarvant, sah?"'

"'There was something quite familiar in both his appearance and his tones, but I couldn't place him till he suddenly cried out in a joyous tone, "Why, sho now, ef it ain't Marse Ormsby! Oh, sah, I'se might, pow'ful glad to see yo'. I cayn't neber fo'git how yo' tried to sabe me an' Rachel and de chill'n from bein' carried back to de house ob bondage."

"'Of course, you have already guessed that it was poor Sam. He had my hand in a vice-like grip and was gazing at me with the most grateful expression, the big tears rolling down his cheeks.

"'I asked how he had come there, and where were Rachel and the children.

"'At that, he shook his head sorrowfully. He had been sold down South, he said—that's how he came to be there—but Rachel and the children he had been compelled to leave behind and had never heard of since. He had half hoped I might be able to give him news of them and sighed with a sad kind of resignation when I told him I had none to give.

"'I was without a body servant, and I need hardly tell you I gladly engaged him in that capacity.'"

"Dat my ole man, Sam!" cried Rachel, "An' he's gwine stay wid Marse Ormsby!"

"Yes, Rachel, as long, I presume, as the fortunes of war permit," said Zillah. "I shall write to the captain today and will gladly send any message for you to Sam. And I hope that when the war is over, my husband and yours will return here together."

Rachel wept for joy. "Oh, bress de Lawd, de good Lawd!" she cried, clasping her hands and lifting streaming eyes to heavn. "Now I'se got hope ob seein' Sam ag'in when dis wah is ober. I'd 'mos' gib up, mistis. Seemed like we's neber gwine meet no mo' till we's bofe pass ober Jordan."

"My poor Rachel, I am very glad for you, and I hope there are many happy days yet in store for you and Sam on this side of Jordan," Mildred said kindly.

"T'ank you, mistis, — t'ank you bofe, good ladies," Rachel responded, curtseying and looking gratefully from one to the other. "Now I mus' be gwine back to my wuk."

"And while you are doing it, you can be thinking what you would like me to say for you to Sam," said Zillah.

"Zillah, dear, I am rejoiced for both you and Rachel," said Mildred. "We are all full of joy that both Wallace and Cyril escaped all the and dangers of that awful battle of Shiloh, or Pittsburg Landing, for they seem to call it by both names."

"Oh, it was an awful battle!" exclaimed Zillah. "And to think that many of our troops had never fired their guns before and, indeed, hardly knew how to load them! It seems perfectly wonderful that they could fight at all under such circumstances. I am sure they deserve any amount of credit, and yet some of the newspapers have called them cowards. It is doubtless very easy for some men to stay at home, out of danger, and abuse as cowards those who are defending them at the front."

"I have just been reading Cyril's letter," said Mildred. "He says a young soldier belonging to an Iowa regiment told him that the first cartridge he ever held in his hands was fired by him at the Rebels in that battle, and that from a rifle which had never been fired from before."

"That regiment," he says, "was one of the first under fire, and though the whole army was being slowly forced back towards the river, by the overwhelming numbers of the Rebels, it never, for the space of two hours, moved from the first line of battle formed by it, and not until it had lost over two hundred in dead and wounded. Then, with its ranks bleeding and broken, it was driven back in confusion but partly reformed, and with the last line on the riverbank, repulsed the almost victorious Rebels in their last charge and slept on the ground that night, in spite of a terrible storm which drenched both friend and foe.

"But let me read from the letter. It is addressed to mother, and Annis brought it in to me, saying that you were to have it afterward. I want to read you this about the battle, and then you shall have the letter to peruse for yourself.

"I want the children to hear it," she added, as at that moment they came in from school. Then she began to read:

"'If that line formed on sabbath evening had been broken, the Army of the Tennessee would have been destroyed, for there was no way to retreat. Let me tell you how that line was formed. Every regiment, every brigade, and every division had been broken, with terrible loss, and driven back to the river. Every battery had lost all, or nearly all, of its guns, and some of the pieces saved

138

were literally torn from the hands of the Rebels. Generals without divisions, and field officers without regiments, exerted themselves, under the direction of Grant, to form a line, out of the broken fragments of the army, on the bluff next the river, to protect the ammunition, subsistence, and the thousands of cowards who covered the bank under the bluff. Stray pieces of artillery, fragments of companies and regiments, in fact, everything that bore a semblance of discipline in the wild confusion, was placed in position. The flag of nearly every regiment in the army was there, with a few of their men. The rest were either dead or wounded, strewn over that six miles of battle, or were proving themselves cravens in the hour of need.

"'Just before dark, upon this line of truly brave men, the Rebels made their last grand charge, which they proudly boasted would force us into the river.

"'They came on, sure of victory, but met such a fire as they had never felt before. They faltered and retreated in confusion. Thus we had gained the first victory in the long agony of that day, and the army was safe, for Buell's force crossed the river that night.

"'The next morning we attacked and, after a half day's hard fighting, drove the Rebels from the field.'"*

"Oh," cried Percy, as his mother ceased reading, "how they must have enjoyed driving the enemy, who had been pressing them so hard! Here, mother, is another letter for you. It must have come by the second mail, I suppose, as I found it in the

---

* Extracts from the letter of a nephew—a young Iowa soldier—who was in the battle.

office on my way home from school. I see it is from Naples, Italy," he added, glancing at the postmark, then handing it to her.

"Yes," she said on seeing the handwriting, "from cousin Rose Dinsmore. I am very glad to hear from her again and learn how they all are."

She tore open the missive and perused it in silence while Zillah was busy with Cyril's. Presently she sighed deeply, and both Zillah and Percy asked if it brought bad news.

"Yes," she replied. "Rose writes that all her brothers enlisted early in the war and that in that dreadful affair at Ball's Bluff, Richard was badly wounded and Freddie was killed. They seem to be feeling as badly about the distracted condition of our common country as we do, but Rose says she cannot be too thankful that they went to Europe before the struggle began and so are not at home in the midst of it."

"They are for the Union?" Zillah said inquiringly.

"Oh, yes! Though at Roselands, all the family— except, perhaps, Walter—are strong for secession."

"Just as I supposed. Well, I presume the friendship between that branch of the family and ourselves is a thing of the past."

"I have no doubt they are at present decidedly hostile in their feelings towards us." assented Mildred. "Yet," she added, "I am not entirely without hope of a renewal of the friendship after this dreadful war is over."

"To what friendship do you allude?" asked her husband, coming in at that moment.

"That of our Dinsmore relatives, not including cousins Horace, Elsie, and their families."

"The others are secessionists, of course," he said.

"Anyone as well acquainted with their characteristics as you and I are would not need to be told so. But you have had some news, I suppose?"

"Yes, letters from Rose and from our soldiers in the Army of the Tennessee," she and Zillah replied, handing them to him.

They left him to their perusal, Zillah going home to attend to her domestic affairs and Mildred into the kitchen to oversee the preparation of a dish which was a special favorite with the doctor.

Much as she was interested in work for the soldiers in field and hospital, and diligent in doing it, she never allowed herself to neglect home duties but always gave them precedence. The welfare and comfort of husband and children she considered her first care, and she had her reward in their devoted affection for her and for each other, and in seeing them healthy and happy.

On returning to the sitting room, she found the doctor in the act of refolding Cyril's letter while wearing the saddest expression she had ever seen on his countenance. "Oh, Milly, my love," he sighed, "what a terrible war this is! Think of that six miles of battlefield strewn with the dead and wounded! Would I could be there to help in caring for the latter and relieving their sufferings!

"But my place still seems to be here. It is not on the battlefield alone, or in the hospital, that those who suffer physically as well as mentally are to be found. Distress over the distracted state of the country is making invalids of many who, before these troubles began, were in health, and greatly aggravating the ailments of such as were already invalids. Indeed, some have died, and others will die, who in ordinary times would have recovered."

"I do not doubt it," said Mildred. "I only wonder that any lover of the country who is without the consolations of God can endure the strain."

"Father, said little Fan, running to him, climbing his knee, and putting her arms lovingly about his neck, "don't look so sorry. God will help us and not let the Union be broken to pieces. I'm going to help a good deal. I'm hemming a handkerchief now for a soldier, and I s'pect I can soon sew on the shirts, 'sides knitting a stocking.

"And I hope there'll be lots of berries on my bushes to make jelly and other nice things for the poor sick soldiers."

"I hope so," he said, caressing her. "Every little bit helps, and if all the children in the country will try as hard as mine do to help the good cause, their efforts will certainly not be without effect, for, as the Scotch say, 'Mony a little mak's a mickle.'"

"We've been working hard for it, father," said Marcia, "and we mean to keep on. We've enlisted for the war."

"Yes," he replied, stroking her hair caressingly as she stood by his side, "but you must allow yourself some recreation. I cannot have you work all the time. Even grown people cannot stand that, much less children."

"No," assented his wife, half remorsefully, "and I fear I have let them do more than I should."

"Mother dear," cried Percy and Marcia in a breath, "you haven't urged us to do anything. We were eager of ourselves to do all we have done."

"Thank you, dears," she answered. "I know you are full of love for the Union and more than willing to exert yourselves to save it, and the knowledge makes your mother proud and happy.

"But come to dinner; it is on the table."

"Milly, my darling," the doctor said to her when they found themselves alone together, "we must try to keep the young hearts of our children from being too much saddened by the turbulence of the times. We can scarcely think of anything else, except when engaged in some employment that must have our thoughts, but, for their sakes, shall we not try to dwell occasionally on brighter themes?"

"Yes," she returned heartily. "I shall do my best to follow out your hint. Youthful days ought to be made bright and joyous. They—my darlings—must not be oppressed with care and labor. I will try to contrive new recreations for them and encourage them to spend more time in play."

"I think Aunt Wealthy will assist you in that," he said. "She is always so bright and cheery."

"Yes, because she so fully obeys the command, 'Be ye therefore followers of God, as dear children,' and has so much of simple, childlike confidence and faith in Him that she seems never to be troubled with doubts or fears and is always satisfied with every allotment of His providence."

These qualities made the old lady greatly beloved, and her arrival early the next month was hailed with delight by all the family connection then in the town.

She made her home with Mr. and Mrs. Keith but passed a great deal of her time with Mildred. But wherever she was, she seemed to be always the same bright, cheery, helpful soul, doing with her might whatsoever her hand found to do, and doing it heartily as to the Lord and not unto men, encouraging others to do likewise—principally by example and occasionally by precept given so lovingly and in a manner so free from any assumption of superior wisdom and goodness that it could not give offense and was almost sure to have the intended effect.

She had a fund of humor, also, and a supply of stories for the children that was well-nigh inexhaustible.

They delighted in gathering about her—particularly in the warm summer evenings when work was done for the day and there was a little time for well-earned rest before going to bed—and then a request for a story was sure to be granted.

She was forgetful and absent-minded, often got her words and sentences mixed up or transposed in a way that was quite droll, but she was so ready to laugh at her own blunders, so free from sensitiveness about the laughter of others, that they were only an added source of amusement.

"Aunt Wealthy," the doctor said to her on one of these occasions, "I think you are about as happy a person as I am acquainted with."

"Probably I am," she returned. "And why shouldn't I be? I am not very young—indeed, I am growing quite old—but I have excellent health, means enough to supply all my own needs and something to spare for others, for the cause of Christ, and for my country. Oh, I have a great many blessings!"

"And are not cursed with the forward heart that findeth no good. Yet I, for one, could not blame you if you were sometimes cast down with anxious thought in regard to our distracted country and the personal danger of a number of those whom you love."

"And so I should be, if I didn't know the blessed truth that God reigns and that nothing can happen to them, to me, or to the land I love without His will; and that His will is always best. I have trusted Him with my eternal interests, and wouldn't it be folly to refuse to trust Him with the temporal? And since He bids me cast all my care on Him and take no thought for the morrow, also to rejoice in Him always, would it not be disobedience and a very great sin to go mourning, fretting, and worrying all my days?"

"You are entirely right," he said. "Your firm faith makes me ashamed of my own doubts and fears. This struggle between the government and rebellion is proving so much more protracted than I had anticipated that my heart sinks within me at times. It does seem that such victories as those of forts Henry and Donelson ought to have brought peace, and I firmly believe they would, had the advantage gained been promptly followed up, leaving no time for the foe to collect new armies and erect new fortifications."

"Yes," she said. "But God is at the helm of our ship of state and will not fail to bring her safely through the breakers in His own good time and way. He will cause the wrath of man to praise him, and the remainder of wrath He will restrain. You may depend, doctor, there is some good to be wrought by these mistakes and delays, though they seem to be only the work of man and very disastrous—perhaps it may be the destruction of slavery."

"That would be worth any amount of treasure," he said, "but, oh, the horrible loss of life! Yes, perhaps even that would be compensated for by the loss of the peculiar institution, for it is a fearful curse to all who are subject to its baneful influence,—the white man even more than the Negro.

"I am a native of that section, grew to manhood there, and I think may be supposed to know whereof I speak."

"Yes," she said, "slavery is a curse, and the Union is a blessing. And I believe that God, in His great goodness and mercy, will destroy the curse and continue the blessing to us and to future generations.

"He is the hearer and answerer of prayer, especially the cry of the oppressed and of him that hath no helper, and for many years these poor downtrodden creatures have been crying to Him for deliverance. Oh, I know it is sure to come!"

It was on a summer evening that the old lady uttered this prophecy, and the next January brought its fulfillment in the President's Emancipation Proclamation.

That caused great joy to the hearts of Sam, away with Capt. Ormsby in the Army of the Tennessee, and Rachel in her kitchen, and to those of millions of others of their race.

# CHAPTER XIV

IT WAS A winter morning. Mildred had seen her husband to the door as he set out upon his daily round among his patients, and now she was busy getting her children off to school, seeing that they were neatly dressed and warmly wrapped up, for the weather was very cold, and preparing a simple lunch for each—a sandwich or two and a little fruit—for taking an early breakfast, they were apt to need something at recess.

Besides, she always made it one of her cares to see that their lessons were well learned and thoroughly understood, especially those of the younger three: Percy was now old enough to attend to his without assistance or oversight, and often to help his brother and sisters if "mother" were too busy.

The door of the dining room, where they all were, opened, and Annis came in, so much more quietly than was her wont that Mildred turned to her in a startled way and at once perceived traces of tears on her cheeks.

"What—what is the matter?" she gasped.

"Rupert has been taken prisoner; he is in that dreadful Libby! Think of him starving there while we are living on the fat of the land!"

Mildred dropped into a chair, pale and trembling, the tears coursing down her cheeks.

"Oh," cried little Fan, "I wish I could give uncle Rupert this nice lunch mother has put up for me!"

"I'd be ever so glad to give him mine," said Marcia. "Mother, can't we pack a big box full of nice things and send it to him?"

"Perhaps we can. I think we must try," she answered, wiping away her tears and endeavoring to assume a cheerful air.

"I have brought his letter," said Annis. "It is to mother and gives an account of his capture."

She unfolded it as she spoke.

"Oh, mother, mother," cried the children in chorus, "mayn't we wait to hear it?"

"Yes," she said, glancing at the clock, "I think there is time. And if I find you are in danger of being late to school in consequence, I will write an excuse."

"Thank you, mother," they returned and sat down ready to listen quietly.

"He dates it "Libby Prison,'" Annis said, then went on to read:

"'Dearest Mother,

"'You will see by my date where I am. I have been here about a week. Fare and accommodations are not exactly what I have been accustomed to at home, but you may comfort yourself with the thought that, for the present, I am in no danger from shot or shell. The hardest thing to me is that I must remain idle while my imperilled country is in sore need of the services of all her sons.

"'But, dear mother, we know that it is all right, since God rules and reigns. "The counsel of the Lord standeth forever, the thoughts of his heart to all generations." And I can plead with Him for the land I love as well in prison as out of it. What a blessing that nothing can come between us and that glorious privilege!

"'I was captured in a mere skirmish, and the fellow who claimed me as his prisoner demanded my boots, ordering me to take them off and give them to him. I declined. They were a new pair of stout cavalry boots, and the prospect of replacing them quite remote.

"'He threatened to shoot me, but I still refused to accede to his demand. Then an officer rode up. The soldier pointed out to him what a desirable pair of boots I had on, and told of his demand, and my refusal.

"'"Pull them off at once, sir," the officer said, addressing me.

"'"I shall do no such thing," I answered. "I am a prisoner or war, and you have no right to rob me of my clothing."

"'"Take them off!" he said threateningly, levelling his pistol at my head.

"'"I will not," I returned.

"'"Then take them from him by force," he said to his men. And I was immediately seized, thrown to the ground, and the boots drawn off my feet and given to the Reb who had demanded them.

"'Then I was marched some miles over a rough, stony road in my stocking feet. Of course, the stockings were soon full of holes, the feet cut, bruised, and bleeding. I could not have gone on had I not been supported by a soldier on each side. I presume if I had not been an officer, I should have been shot down.

"'That painful march over, I was put on board a

train of cars and brought here, the journey consuming two days and a night. And all the food I had during that time was about four square inches of cornbread and a small bit of meat that was just ready to run away.

"'The fare here is on a par with that,* but we— my fellow prisoners and I—are hoping for a speedy exchange. It would be most welcome on several accounts. I am barefooted and have no change of raiment. I comfort myself under these inconveniences by thinking of Washington and his troops in that winter at Valley Forge. Probably my condition is no worse, perhaps not so bad, as was that of those suffering patriot soldiers.

"'I know your first impulse, on reading this, will be to send me what I need of clothing and such other things as would carry this distance. Whether an effort to do so would be successful or not, I cannot say. I think it doubtful but leave it with you to decide whether it is worthwhile to make the trial.

"'But don't be too anxious about your prisoner boy, or let his condition rob you of rest or peace of mind. You know he has with him an all-powerful Friend, who is yours also, and to whom you can speak for him whenever you will. And comfort yourself, dearest mother, with that blessed assurance of His word, "We know that all things work together for good to them that love God."'"

The letter concluded with loving messages to all the dear ones at home.

"Poor, dear boy!" Mildred said, wiping the tears from her eyes. "Of course it is worthwhile to make

* Experiences of a cousin of the writer during the war.

every effort to relieve his sufferings and supply his wants. We will pack a box and send it off this very day, and if that reaches him, it can be followed by another, for if more is sent than he can use for himself, he will share with his fellow prisoners."

"I have a gold eagle father gave me on my last birthday," said Percy. "I will send that to uncle Rupert."

"And I have a five-dollar gold piece—a half-eagle—and I will send it to him," Marcia said eagerly. "And, mother, you know I've just finished knitting a pair of those warm woolen stockings—can't I send them?"

"Yes, dear, they will be very acceptable, and we will send half a dozen pair or more, among us."

"He must have boots, too," said Annis. "I think he left his measure with the shoemaker here. But we can't wait to have a pair made," she added rather ruefully.

"No," Mildred said, "but, knowing the measure, we can get a pair ready made."

"Oh, I wished I'd saved up some of my money, so that I could send it to uncle Rupert!" said Stuart disconsolately. "But I've given and spent till it's all gone. I'd send him my new mittens, but they wouldn't be big enough. Oh! I know what I'll do, if you'll let me, mother. I'll send him my new knife. It's a real good one, with four blades."

Mildred smiled lovingly on her little son when she heard that, for well she knew that the knife in question was one of his greatest treasures.

"Yes, my dear boy," she replied, "that will be a very suitable and useful gift. There may be times when your uncle will find it more valuable to him than money, and the rest of us can send him quite as much of that as the Rebels are at all likely to allow him to receive."

"Mother, what can I send to uncle Rupert?" asked little Fan.

"I will send him the shirt you hemmed the other day, darling, and pin a note to it, telling him that your small fingers did so much of the work. And I know he will enjoy wearing it all the more because his little girl helped to make it," Mildred said. She added, "But now, dears, hurry away to school or you will be too late."

They obeyed and Mildred, turning to Annis, asked, "Does Zillah know?"

"Yes. She ran over just in time to hear the first reading of the letter. She knew of it because it was her Stuart who brought it from the office.

"We all said at once, just as you did, that a box must be sent, and as I came here, Zillah went home to gather up what she could find for it."

"That is good," Mildred said. "It will be packed at father's, of course, and I will at once collect what is to go from here and carry it over there."

"Yes, do," Annis answered. "I'll not wait for you, as I may be needed at home, but you follow me as soon as you can. I presume the box is there by this time, for father went right down to the stores to look for one, and I must help mother in collecting and preparing what we are to put in it."

No time was lost, and by noon a tolerably large box was packed, marked, and on its way to the express office.

It contained all that was needed to supply Rupert Keith's most pressing wants: warm clothing, money, a few books to while away the tedious hours of prison life, some groceries, and delicacies from the well-stored pantries of his mother and sisters.

They counted the days to the time when he might possibly receive their good gifts, and their hearts were not a little comforted with the thought of the relief and enjoyment he would experience in their use.

They were planning to send another box when a letter came, in which they read:

"Your box reached Libby Prison safely, was brought in and set down before me, opened, and its contents shown me. I saw that you, in your love and kindness, had provided abundantly for all my necessities: plenty of warm, decent clothing, many comforts in the way of eatables, money with which to purchase more when that supply should be exhausted, books for my mental enjoyment. All these were taken out and shown me, then returned to the box with the information that I could have none of them, and it was carried immediately away, never to greet my hungry eyes again.* So, dear mother, father, and sisters, do not send anything more, because that would be only to aid and comfort the enemy."

---

* From the Libby Prison experience of a young friend.

# CHAPTER XV

BOOM! MARCIA WOKE at the sound, from a dream of standing upon a hilltop and overlooking the battle which for the last two or three days had been raging at Gettysburg, the news of its progress coming over the wire to Pleasant Plains.

She started up in bed and rubbed her eyes, for a moment bewildered to find herself safe and at home in her own cozy bedroom. Then, as wide-awake consciousness fully returned, she said half aloud, "Oh, it's only the beginning of the usual Fourth of July firing! I'm glad it doesn't mean killing people here."

Slipping from the bed, she ran to the window and looked out.

The sun had just risen above the treetops, and the river was sparkling in his bright beams.

"It's such a lovely day," she thought, "and we're likely to have a pleasant time with our own little private celebration that father and mother have planned so nicely and thoughtfully for us children. Yet how it spoils one's enjoyment to think of poor, dear uncle Rupert in that horrid Confederate prison, uncle Don wounded and in the hospital, and uncle Cyril and uncle Wallace fighting at

Vicksburg! I wonder if they'll ever come back — all of them, or any of them!"

At that moment, a quick, springing step came round the corner of the house. She recognized it and, leaning out, called softly,

"Percy!"

He stepped back and lifted a radiant face to hers. "Oh, I'm glad somebody's awake to hear the glorious news!" he cried. "Victory — a great victory at Gettysburg! But," and the brightness of his face clouded somewhat, "it has been an awful, awful struggle. Splendid fighting on both sides and thousands upon thousands of brave men killed and wounded, Federals and Confederates both."

"Oh, then," she responded, "how many, many people are in terrible pain this lovely Fourth of July morning! It almost spoils the news and everything to think of that."

"Yes, but we should be very thankful because the bigger the victories and the more of them, the sooner the war will be over."

"Oh, Percy, it has lasted so long!"

"Yes, two years, but the Revolution lasted between seven and eight. So we mustn't be discouraged."

"But our armies are so much larger, and so many more people are killed and wounded in one battle!"

"That is true, but I feel quite sure it won't last nearly as long as the Revolution did.

"Oh, mother, good morning," he said as another face appeared beside Marcia's. "I've been downtown to learn the news, and it is of a great victory at Gettysburg."

"Oh, I am glad and thankful!" she said. "Surely, surely we shall have peace before long. I must tell your father." And she hurried back to her room, where her husband, who had just risen, was preparing for the day.

"It is cause for great thankfulness," he said when he had heard her tidings, "to God first, then to the brave fellows who have fought so long and determinedly to save Pennsylvania from invasion. What a terrific struggle it has been! And, oh, the awful suffering thousands are at this moment enduring in consequence! That is one thing a great victory means."

"Yes," she sighed, "my heart bleeds for the wounded, the new-made widows and orphans on both sides. Those leaders of the rebellion, whose unholy ambition has brought about this terrible state of affairs, must have hearts of stone if they ever know happiness or peace of mind again.

"I do not feel at all inclined for merrymaking today, but, for the children's sake, the plans for their enjoyment must be carried out. Do you not think so?"

"I do, indeed," he answered. "To shut out pleasure from their young lives and sadden their hearts would be of no assistance to the cause of the Union. Nor will it help it for us to court gloom and sadness. Let us be as cheerful as we can, Milly love, at the same time that we give all the sympathy and help that it is in our power to bestow to those who are in sorrow or pain."

The town looked festive on that bright summer morning, flags flying from nearly every house, while cannon were booming at intervals in honor of the day and the victory. And before night, news of another — the surrender of Vicksburg — added to the general joy.

Yet deep sadness for near and dear ones killed or wounded, or the uncertainty in regard to the fate of others, filled many and many a heart almost to the exclusion of the joy and exultation which would otherwise been have felt in the success of the Federal arms.

A family picnic had been planned by our friends principally for the enjoyment of the children and young people, and a lovely spot on the riverbank some distance below the town had been chosen for the purpose. And soon after an early breakfast, they all repaired there, some going in carriages by the road, others down the river in a rowboat propelled by Stuart Ormsby and Percy Landreth.

Those two were now well-grown lads of sixteen, Stuart the elder by a few months, and the task was no difficult one for their strong young arms.

Percy owned the boat, a birthday gift from his father, and he and his brother and cousin had had many an hour of enjoyment in rowing for miles up and down the swiftly flowing, beautiful stream.

Jim was dispatched first to the place of rendezvous with a wagon carrying a table, camp chairs, and baskets of provisions, and when the others arrived, they found comfortable seats ready for them on the green grass in the shade of forest trees.

The ladies had brought their knitting (stockings for the soldiers); the little girls, their dolls; and the boys, fishing tackle.

Mr. Keith, the only gentleman of the party till the doctor could join them after making his round, had the morning papers with him and read the news to the ladies and such of the young folks as were sufficiently interested to care to hear.

Then the boys caught some fish, made a fire, and cooked them, thus providing an agreeable addition to the dainties brought from home.

After dinner the younger children gathered about Aunt Wealthy begging for a story—a request which she kindly granted, nor did she refuse when another and yet another were called for.

Stuart Ormsby and Percy listened for a time but at length stole away and wandered along the riverbank together.

They were quite out of sight and hearing of the others when they reached a fallen tree and sat down upon it for a talk.

It was Stuart who spoke first.

"Percy, I've about made up my mind to enlist, instead of going to college with you in the fall, if I can get father and mother to consent."

"And I have come to the very same resolution," returned his cousin. "Though I have but little hope of gaining consent or that boys of our age would be accepted, though we hear that, in the South, they are filling up their ranks with even younger ones."

"Well, we can but try. And as the folks are all together now, under the trees yonder, suppose we go back at once and ask consent."

"Agreed! Who shall be spokesman?"

"You, if you like, as you are the eldest."

"Very well, and, if there's any necessity, you may help me out with all the eloquence at your command."

With that, they rose and retraced their steps, drawing near the group under the trees in a manner so excited as to instantly attract the attention of all.

"What is it, Stuart?" asked his mother. "Has anything gone wrong?"

"No, mother, it is only that Percy and I think it is time we were doing something for our country in her time of need, and we have come to ask leave to enlist."

"Oh, my boy, you are much too young!" she said quickly, her cheek paling as she spoke. "Besides, I could not give you permission without first learning your father's will in the matter."

Percy was looking at his parents, seated close together. He saw that his mother's eyes were full of tears, his father's of mingled pride, love, and pain.

"My son," he said, a trifle huskily, "I am proud of your willingness to sacrifice yourself upon the altar of your country, and if you were a year or two older, my consent should not be withheld for a moment. But you are too young, and growing too rapidly, to have strength to endure the long marches and other hardships of a soldier's life in time of war. You must wait, my boy, at least another year. And Stuart should, I think, do likewise."

"I am sure your father is right, Percy," said their grandfather. "I, too, am proud of your willingness to go to fight your country's battles but couldn't consent to see you try it while you are so young and there are plenty of men to fill up the ranks."

"And, oh, I hope the war will not last till they are fit for enlistment!" said Zillah. "I feel as if I had done enough in giving up my husband and all my brothers to the cause."

"Still, mother, I am sure you will not withhold your only son if he should be needed in another year or two," Stuart said with an affectionate look.

She did not reply; her heart was too full. But the doctor said,

"Don't let us trouble ourselves with the question

now, for 'sufficient unto the day is the evil thereof,' and the war may be over before the year is out."

So the matter was settled for the time, and the boys gave themselves to their studies with redoubled zeal, thinking they might be obliged to resign them the next year, for at least a time, should the war continue.

A few weeks later, Rupert, now Colonel Keith, came home a paroled prisoner, his wife with him.

The joy of reunion with parents, sisters, and friends was very great, and the stories he had to tell of his campaigns and his experiences in hospital and prison were eagerly listened to by old and young.

He had left them a healthy, robust man. He returned pale, thin, weak, and with a hacking cough that caused them great alarm. But it soon disappeared, and he recuperated rapidly under the tender care and nursing of wife and mother, pure air, and well-cooked, wholesome food, which were a most agreeable change from the tainted atmosphere and wretched fare of Libby Prison.

It was a positive delight to his mother and sisters to set him down to a well-spread board and see his enjoyment of its dainties.

One evening shortly after his return, seated on the porch at his father's with the whole family gathered about him, he told of his Fourth spent in the prison, and how he had thought of them all at home and knew they were thinking of him.

"I was very homesick that day," he said, "and I am pretty certain that everyone of the three hundred Federal officers then in the Libby felt about as I did.

"I can assure you, that when, on the morning of

the sixth, we heard that a flag-of-truce boat had arrived at City Point for the purpose of conveying Federal prisoners to Annapolis, we were an almost jubilant set of fellows, for we thought we were all about to be exchanged or released on parole.

"That good news was presently followed by an order for all the captains to report in one of the lower rooms. That raised our hopes still higher, for we thought they were ordered down for the purpose of being paroled, preparatory to being taken to the boat, and that the rest of us would soon follow.

"You may be sure we were in a state of great excitement and anxiety while we waited for over an hour for their return or some information as to what had become of them.

"Well, at last the door opened, and they filed in—all but two of them—but we saw at once that a great change had come over them. They had left us full of hope, in high spirits, but they came back gloomy and sad.

"Of course, questions were showered upon them as to where they had been and what had happened to work so great a change in them.

"They told us, in reply, that, when they reached the room, they were ordered to—the commandant of the prison told them that he had a very painful duty to perform, that he had been ordered to have them draw lots to determine which two of them should be hung in retaliation for the death of two Confederate captains whom Burnside had captured some months before and summarily executed as spies.

"That he then wrote the name of each on a slip of paper, deposited the slips in a box, and said they might select one of their own number to draw out two of them, and those whose names should be found on them would be the ones who were to die by hanging."

"Oh, uncle," cried Fan, "I'm so glad you'd quit being a captain before that!"

"Are you, my pet?" he said, drawing her to his side and putting his arm round her waist. "Well, I acknowledge that I was not sorry myself."

"Oh, uncle! Tell the rest, won't you, please?" exclaimed Ada Ormsby. "Did they choose one to draw the lots? And did he do it?"

"They consulted together and chose the chaplain of the Fifth Maryland Infantry to draw the lots. So he was sent for and consented to do it."

"You may be sure, children, it was a very solemn business. Think of all those poor fellows standing looking on, thinking, 'Perhaps the lot may fall on me, and I have to die that ignominious death.'

"You remember I told you that when the captains came back to us, two of their number were missing? They were Capt. Henry W. Sawyer of the First New Jersey Cavalry and Capt. John D. Flinn of the First Indiana Infantry, the men who had drawn the prize of death.

"They were taken to General Winder's headquarters, where sentence of death by hanging was formally passed upon them, to be carried out at some time and place to be named by Jefferson Davis, the Confederate president.

"Then they were brought back to the prison and confined in cells for some days. After that, they were allowed to join the rest of us through the day but were put in the cells again at night."

"Oh, uncle! And have they been hung?" cried the children.

"No, not yet, and I don't think they will be. Fortunately, our government holds some Confederate officers prisoners, and on hearing of this affair, believing the condemnation of Sawyer and Flinn groundless and unjust, they immediately ordered Gen. Fitzhugh Lee and Captain Winder, a son of General Winder, into close confinement and informed the Confederate authorities that if Sawyer and Flinn were executed, Lee and Winder should suffer death in the same manner. Since hearing that, they have thought best to treat the two condemned captains as they do the other Federal prisoners."*

* Gen. R. S. Northcott, in *Philadelphia Weekly Times*. "After this, but little was ever heard of the matter. The day of execution was never named by the Confederate president. Sawyer and Flinn were paroled with others, and sent to Annapolis, by flag-of-truce boat, on the 14th of March, 1864."

# CHAPTER XVI

"TELL US SOMETHING more, uncle, won't you?" entreated little Fan, — "something that happened to your own self."

"Yes," he said, "I was just thinking of a very narrow escape from death that I had, though I knew nothing about it at the time.

"It was at a time when Federals and Confederates were so near together that there was almost constant skirmishing between the pickets.

"There had been a good deal of that through the day, and I had been in the saddle from early dawn. The weather was cold and raw, and I felt stiff and weary. I had been out on a reconnaissance and in returning had carelessly allowed myself to become separated from my command. But now, being within our own picket line, I felt in no particular danger and, dismounting, gathered some brush and started a fire to warm my benumbed hands and stiffened limbs. But, just as it blazed up, I thought of the very possible proximity of some Rebel sharpshooter and hastily extinguished it.

"The idea of danger lurking near brought with it the compensating thought of that almighty, ever-present Friend, without whom not a sparrow shall fall on the ground, and I sang,

> *"Cover my defenseless head*
> *With the shadow of Thy wing!'*

"Some weeks later, a fit of sickness caused me to be sent to the hospital for a brief period. A Confederate officer, who had been wounded and taken prisoner, lay in the next cot to mine, and I noticed with some surprise that he frequently gazed very earnestly and searchingly at me.

"I wondered what it was about me that excited his curiosity, but I asked no questions and, indeed, tried not to seem to be aware of his scrutiny, till he one day suddenly addressed me, asking if I had not done the very thing I have just been telling you of—started a fire on such a night, in such a locality, and as suddenly extinguished it, at the same time singing,

> *"Cover my defenseless head*
> *With the shadow of Thy wing!'*

"I answered that I had done so, then asked, 'But how is it that you knew of that heedless act?'

"'Because I was near enough at the time to both see and hear you,' he said. 'Standing back in the darkness of the wood, the sudden blazing up of your fire attracted my attention, showed me that you wore the uniform of a Federal officer, and gave me a distinct view of your face. You were within easy pistol range. I took aim at you and had my finger on the trigger when you began to sing that stanza from Wesley's hymn, so familiar and dear to every Christian heart in the English-speaking world.'

"'I felt at once that we were brethren in Christ, though belonging to opposing armies, and it was impossible to take your life.'"

"What a good Providence it was that led you to sing those words!" said Rupert's mother, grateful tears shining in her eyes.

"Yes," said Aunt Wealthy, "but how strange it must seem to the angels to see Christian men fighting and killing each other! There can't be a doubt that there are many good men on both sides."

"No," said Rupert, "and there is wonderfully little enmity felt, except by the leaders of the secession movement, the men who brought about the conflict by persistent falsehood and misrepresentation.

"See, in proof of what I say, how the victors and vanquished fraternized immediately upon the surrender of Vicksburg, our troops witnessing the marching out and stacking of arms by the vanquished without a cheer, seeming to feel sadness for them in their humiliation, rather than exultation over their defeat. And how, on entering the city, they at once began feeding them from their own haversacks.

"I, for one, feel very hopeful," he went on. "Those two recent victories at Vicksburg and Gettysburg have broken the backbone of the rebellion, and though we may have much hard fighting before us, still the ultimate triumph of the government is assured."

"Yes," assented Dr. Landreth, "those two successes lifted a great load from every loyal heart, from that of the President down to private citizens like ourselves."

As health and strength were regained, the war still continuing, Colonel Keith grew anxious and impatient to be in the field again, but it was not until the following spring that circumstances permitted the carrying out of his wish.

One day in March, Percy came hurrying in with the exclamation, "News, mother, several items of it!"

"What?" she asked, her heart beating fast as she glanced up into his excited face.

"First, that Grant is made lieutenant general and given command of all the armies of the United States."

"Ah, that is good news, Percy," Mildred returned emphatically.

He went on, "The second is that uncle Rupert has been exchanged and is ordered back to his regiment."

Mildred sighed. "It is what he has been wishing for," she remarked, her voice slightly tremulous.

"Yes, mother, he is glad. But grandma and my aunts, though they say nothing against it, seem hardly able to keep their tears back. Aunt Juanita goes with him as far as Philadelphia, or perhaps Washington.

"Now for my last item of news. It is that a letter was received this morning from uncle Wallace, and in it he gives Cousin Stuart leave to enlist."

He paused, but she knew that he had not said all that he wished to. She looked up at him with eyes swimming in tears and rapidly paling cheek.

"What else, Percy?" she asked, vainly trying to steady her tones.

"Mother, dear, the year my father spoke of has nearly passed by, and I think my country needs me. Father has said I, too, may enlist, if I can win my mother's consent."

A moment's struggle with herself, a swift, silent petition sent up to a throne of grace for the fulfillment of the gracious promise, "As thy days, so shall thy strength be." Then, giving him a look of fond, fond mother love and pride, she said, "My boy, if you hear the call of your country, go. Your mother will never stand in your way, and I think I need not warn you never to disgrace her or yourself by a show of cowardice."

"God helping me, I will not, mother," he said earnestly. "But, having not yet girded on my harness, I dare not boast myself as he that putteth it off. But I shall be continually asking for grace and strength to do my duty as a brave soldier and patriot, and I shall know that my mother and all the dear ones at home are helping me with their prayers."

"Yes," she said with emotion, "there will not be an hour of the day in which my heart will not be going up to the Hearer and Answerer of prayer, on behalf of the dear son of my love, my first-born, that the God of his fathers may cover his head in the day of battle and preserve him from all evil."

He knelt by her side and clasped her in his arms.

"Mother, mother! Best and dearest of mothers!" he said, his voice growing husky. "The very hardest part is leaving you—leaving you and not knowing that I shall ever see your sweet face again."

"My boy! My dear, dear boy!" she said, laying her head on his shoulder while the tears began to fall thick and fast. "You have been the comfort and blessing of my life since the day you were born. To lose you out of it would be worse than death, yet I freely give you to my country in her hour of need. But, oh, God grant you may be restored to me again!"

For another moment she allowed herself to rest in the strong young arms enfolding her so tenderly, while he fondly caressed her hair and cheek, his heart going up in an ardent petition that, when the feebleness of age should come upon her, he might be near to be her stay and staff. Then she roused herself.

"This is no time for the indulgence of useless grief and lamentation," she said gently withdrawing from his embrace and wiping away her tears. "I must be getting you ready for your journey, and I suppose the time is short?"

"Yes, mother, only two days if we go with uncle, as we would prefer."

"It is perhaps just as well," she sighed. "Delay would but prolong the agony of parting."

With that she set to work at once to put his clothing in thorough order and prepare every comfort that he could carry with him.

There was little or no leisure for sad forebodings; there was time only to think of and provide for his needs, to besiege a throne of grace on his behalf, and to try to fortify him against temptation with wise, loving, motherly counsel.

Always affectionate and helpful, he was even more so than his wont during those two days, lingering at her side whenever he could, giving any assistance in his power, and eagerly listening to every word that fell from her lips.

"Percy, my dear, dear son," she said in her last talk with him before he left, "never forget that you are, first of all, a soldier of Jesus Christ and as such must be ready to endure hardness in His

service. Never be afraid or ashamed to acknowledge Him as the Captain of your salvation, the
One in whom you trust, and whose commands you
are bound to obey.

"There may be times when you will find it
requires more courage to do that than to march up
to the cannon's mouth."

"Yes, mother, I believe that," he replied. "But oh,
I trust that I shall never be left to deny Him or do
anything to bring reproach upon His cause!"

"I fear you will be exposed to many and great
temptations," she said. "You will doubtless see much
of drunkenness and vice in other forms. Your ears
will be often assailed by profanity—oh, let it never
defile your lips! You have no vices now; God grant
you may not come back to me as pure as you go!

"But if I did not believe more than that you are
free from vice, I could not let you go. I do believe
that you are, as you profess to be, a true child of
God and that He will keep you in all your ways.
He says to you, as to Joshua of old,

"'I will not fail thee, nor forsake thee. Be strong
and of a good courage.'

"Remember also the command which follows:

"'This book of the law shall not depart out of thy
mouth; but thou shalt meditate therin day and
night, that thou mayest observe to do according to
all that is written therein: for then thou shalt have
good success. Have not I commanded thee? Be
strong and of a good courage; be not afraid, neither
be thou dismayed: for the Lord thy God is with
thee whithersoever thou goest.'"

"What great and precious promises, mother!" he
said. "I shall try to keep them in my memory, to
treasure them up in my heart. I remember the

psalmist says, 'Thy word have I hid in my heart, that I might not sin against thee.'

"And I am sure the knowledge that my mother at home is praying for me, will be a great safeguard in the hour of temptation."

"And, my son, remember that it is not enough that you have enlisted in the Lord's service yourself but you must try to bring others to Him. It is not enough that you are enjoying the gospel feast, you are to invite others to partake with you.

"'Let him that heareth say, Come.'

"If you are looking for opportunities to speak a word for the Master, and to do good to the souls and bodies of your fellow men, you will not fail to find them. Ask God for wisdom and strength for this work, as well as for what you are called to do in saving the Union from destruction.

"We are to take Christ for our example, and He went about doing good. He that wins souls is wise. 'And they that be wise shall shine as the brightness of the firmament; and they that turn many to righteousness as the stars for ever and ever.'"

"Oh, that is worth striving for!" he said. "And, mother, it is my ardent desire, my most earnest purpose, so to live and act and speak so that all who come in contact with me may recognize me as a follower of Jesus.

"It would greatly distress me to hear that anyone who had had an opportunity to judge of me by my life had expressed surprise on learning that I professed to be such."

"That is as I would have you feel," she replied, "for the Master says, 'Let your light so shine before men, that they may see your good works, and glorify your Father which is in heaven.'"

The parting counsels given Percy by his father and grandparents were in much the same strain, for it was the great desire of all their hearts that he should prove himself a true soldier of the cross as well as of the government.

Some years before this, he had become a communicant member of the church to which his parents belonged and had led a very consistent life. He was a most lovable young man, and all his relatives felt it a trial to see him depart to face the hardships and dangers of war.

Next to his mother, his sister Marcia, perhaps, felt it most severely, for Percy was almost an idol with her, while she—now a sweet, fair girl just budding into womanhood—was scarcely less dear to him.

When the time for parting came, she clung about his neck, weeping as if her heart would break, seeming as if she could never let him go.

He held her close for a brief space, then had to tear himself away.

Fan came next, and it was almost equally difficult to release himself from her loving, weeping embrace.

Then for a moment he and Stuart were locked in each other's arms, then his father's were about him, while in tones trembling with strong emotion he blessed his first-born son and sought for him the protecting care of the God of battles.

His mother's kiss was the last imprinted upon his lips, his cheek, his brow, as she strained him to her heart with emotion too deep for words.

"Mother, mother! Dear, dearest mother!" he faltered. "Oh, may God bless you and keep you, and let me see your sweet face again!"

Then she found words. "Dear child, we shall meet again," she said, "if not here, hereafter. But I feel that you will be restore to me again, even in this world. And I am proud of my brave soldier boy, who so loves his native land that he is willing to risk life and limb for her salvation."

Zillah's parting with her son was not less tender and affecting, or less brave, and the sisters found no little consolation in their mutual sympathy and love.

Yet they did not waste time and energy in weeping and lamentation, but with resolute cheerfulness, they gave both to the cause of their country, doing with their might whatsoever their hands found to do for her, while at the same time their hearts were often going up in prayer for her, for their sons, and for all who were suffering or in peril for her sake.

They were no longer troubled with any fear that the final issue of the struggle might not be for the government. But there was still much to fear and dread for their loved ones, much in the reports of the sufferings of the wounded and of Federal prisoners in Rebel hands to wring their hearts. And many a time would they have failed within them, had they not been able to stay them upon the God of Israel.

Oh, with what trembling and apprehension, with what a cry for help to endure whatever might be in store for them, would they scan the columns of the newspaper or open a letter from the seat of war! Yet, always, they found the promise fulfilled, "As they days, so shall thy strength be." As they afterward testified — when peace had come — never once did it fail.

"Many are the afflictions of the righteous: but the Lord delivereth him out of them all."

And "our light affliction, which is but for a moment, worketh for us a far more exceeding and eternal weight of glory."

# CHAPTER XVII

THE BOYS WROTE to their mothers as frequently and fully as circumstances would permit, often giving graphic descriptions of the life they were leading, the battles they witnessed or participated in, but making light of their hardships and dwelling hopefully upon the prospect that the end of the struggle was drawing nigh.

They were greatly missed at home, and their letters were always hailed with delight yet opened with trembling, lest they should contain news of disaster to the writers or the cause of the Union.

Mildred was very happy in her children. They were all so devoted to both her and their father; so kind, respectful, and dutiful; so anxious to do everything in their power to save her from vexation, care, toil, and trouble of every description.

Marcia was already capable of taking the oversight of household affairs and did so far as her mother would permit. But Mildred, while rejoicing in her daughter's capability, was by no means willing to have her overburdened with labors and responsibilities too heavy for her years. She and the doctor were fully agreed in the desire to prepare their children to meet successfully the duties and responsibilities that must come upon them sooner or later and yet to make life as bright and joyous as possible for them in their youthful days under the parental roof.

Stuart, though perhaps less gifted than his older brother, was quite as dutiful, affectionate, industrious, and conscientious, always faithful in attending to anything required of him or undertaken of his own free will. If he could not master a subject with the same ease that Percy did, he never shirked the plodding necessary to enable him to finally reach the desired end.

The brothers had an earnest talk before Percy left, in which the elder entreated the younger to try to supply his place to their parents during his absence, and the younger readily promised to do so to the utmost of his ability.

Percy was satisfied, for Stuart's word, once given, was sure to be kept. He was only thirteen but had as much steadiness of character, and was as fully to be relied upon, as though he had seen twice that number of years.

As bedtime approached, on the evening after Percy went, Stuart quietly remarked to his mother that he had arranged to take his brother's duties.

"And now, if you will trust me, mother," he concluded, "I shall lock up the house."

"My dear boy," she said with a half-tearful, smiling look into his grave, earnest face, "I esteem you quite as worthy of trust as your brother, and that, you know, is saying a good deal."

"Yes, indeed, mother! And thank you for it. Of course, I cannot hope to do things quite so well as he did, but I'm resolved to do my very best. If I were a man, I'd like to go and help fight for the

Union, but as I can't do that, I'll try to help by filling the place of one who has gone."

"Some must stay at home," said Marcia, "and, even if you were old enough to go, it would hardly be fair to expect mother and father to give up both their sons."

"It would be very hard for me to do that," acknowledged Mildred, "but some others have done still more. I read in the papers the other day of a widow who had six sons and sent them all—and, terrible to relate, they have all been killed but one, and he is wounded. Poor, poor woman! How she endures it I cannot tell! I hope she is a Christian and knows that her sons trusted in Christ and that the separation is only for a time, for I am sure nothing less—nothing else—could comfort under such an affliction."

"How glad I am that we have that to comfort us in thinking about Percy!" Marcia said, wiping away the tears which were falling fast from her eyes. "I wish all our soldiers were Christians. And, oh, mother, I wish I could do something worthwhile to help save the Union! I feel that Percy is doing so, but I am only a girl and can't fight."

"No, but you can pray for the cause as well as for our dear ones who are giving themselves to it, and it has been well said that 'prayer moves the Arm that moves the universe.' No one is required to do more than he or she can, and it will be enough if it shall be said of us at the last, 'She hath done what she could.'"

While they talked, Stuart had been going round securing doors and windows.

Coming back, he said, "Now, mother, everything is fast for the night, and in the morning I'll be up early and see to father's office—put it in good order—and that Jim takes proper care of the horses, attends to the fires, and does all his chores."

"Jim's older than you are and ought not to need you to look after him," remarked Marcia with a slightly amused smile.

"No, and I suppose he means to do about right. But of course he doesn't take the same interest in matters that I do, and he's heedless and needs to be looked after. It's like it is with you and Rachel: She's an excellent cook and faithful about her work, yet you look after her and give her directions sometimes when mother is too busy to do it."

"Yes, and you are both very helpful to me," said Mildred, glancing affectionately from one to the other. "My children are all great blessings to their father and mother."

The months rolled on: July had come and nearly gone again, when Miss Stanhope received a letter form her nephew, Harry Duncan.

Her face lighted up with pleasure, and she breathed a sigh of thankfulness as it was handed to her, for it was the first in many months, and she was growing very anxious for the young man's safety.

Though he wrote in a lively strain, trying to jest and make merry over his privations and sufferings endured in his country's cause, her tears fell fast as she read, and she said to herself that the truth, had she known it, would have been scarcely less distressing than she had found the suspense.

Much of the time had been filled up, for him and his comrades, with hard fighting, long, wearisome marches through heat and cold, mud and rain and snow, or under a scorching summer sun. Often they had slept upon the bare ground, sometimes with no covering but the sky, not seldom faring hardly, occasionally going hungry because the enemy had succeeded in seizing or destroying military stores. Yet all this was as nothing compared to the sufferings endured in Andersonville, where he had been for a time imprisoned.

"I can give you no conception of the horrors of the place," he wrote. "It seemed to me a veritable hell upon earth, so full of filth and stench, of the dead and the dying, of men crazed with the agonies of thirst and starvation and exposure to heat and cold, the biting frosts of winter and the scorching suns of summer alike, for they have not the slightest shelter except as they burrow in the ground.

"And they are guarded on every side by fiends in human shape who seem to revel in their sufferings and add to them at every opportunity, shooting them down upon the slightest pretext, so slight as the accidental laying of a hand upon the dead line. And to this they are urged on by a promised reward of thirty days' furlough for every Federal prisoner shot.

"Many and great as are the prisoners' causes of distress, the greatest is from thirst. A stream of water flows directly across the enclosure, but it is green, slimy, sluggish, polluted with all the filth of the sewerage from the village of Andersonville and of the Rebel camp, which is placed above instead of below the prison.

"The only water fit to drink comes from a spring beyond the eastern wall, flowing under it and emptying into the other a few feet from the dead line. The supply is not nearly sufficient for the thousands of prisoners crowded into that horrible enclosure who must drink or die, so that there is always a throng about the spot. And as the men press upon each other in their effort to get to the water to quench their raging thirst, some are inevitably pushed upon the dead line, then the sharp crack of a rifle is sure to be heard, and the poor unfortunate is sent into eternity.

"But I will not harrow your feelings with any more of this. I was so fortunate as to escape after a few days' imprisonment there, and to bring away with me a brother of Horace Dinsmore's wife — Harold Allison, who, poor fellow, had been there so long and suffered so terribly that he is not likely ever to recover his health, or even to live many months.

"Some others escaped with us, and we accomplished it by digging a well and then tunnelling through to some distance beyond the wall."

Of course, Aunt Wealthy shared the reading of her letter with the rest. Their sympathies were strongly aroused for the poor prisoners by it and also by newspaper accounts of the heart-rending condition of many returned prisoners from Andersonville, which were published about that time.

They hoped that none whom they knew and loved were sharing the horrors of that fearful place, but their petitions went up, night and day, for the relief and rescue of all who were shut up within its walls.

One day in the fall, a letter came for Mildred, from Don's wife.

She had written some weeks before that she had been without news of him for a much longer time than usual and was growing very uneasy.

In this, she said he had come home a paroled prisoner from Andersonville and in so pitiable a condition that it nearly broke her heart to look at him, though he affirmed that he had escaped well indeed, in comparison with many others. And the doctor said there was a possibility of his entire recovery, though he feared the bad effects would remain, to some extent, for the rest of his life.

It was sorrowful news to mother, father, and sisters, yet far from being so terrible as if the tidings had been that he was still in captivity.

They wrote at once, earnestly entreating him to visit his childhood's home as soon as he had strength for the journey.

The invitation was gladly accepted, and when Thanksgiving Day came round again, he, his wife and children were there to share in its festivities.

It was not so joyous an occasion as that former one, when Mr. and Mrs. Keith were able to gather about them all their children and grandchildren, for the war was still in progress, and two sons and two grandsons were exposed to its dangers.

Still, their hearts were filled with thankfulness that things were no worse with them, that, so far as they knew, the absent dear ones were not killed, wounded, or in captivity.

Don, glancing over the table loaded with the delicacies of the season, remarked with emotion, "What a contrast this is to the meals served out to me and my fellow prisoners three months ago! How thankful I should have been then for a full meal of this bread alone, or these potatoes! Yes, for half a meal or for one glass of pure, cold water such as this," he said, pointing to a tumbler that stood beside his plate.

"Do tell us, uncle, what had you to eat?" questioned Ada Ormsby.

He replied, "One week's daily rations consisted of one pint of meal composed of cob and corn ground up together, half a pint of peas full of bugs, and four ounces of mule meat, generally spoiled and emitting an odor which—to say the least—was not delightful."

"And what on the alternate week?" asked the doctor, his eyes kindling with indignation while the others looked as if their hearts were too full for speech.

"The same, except that instead of meal, we had four square inches of cornbread."

"Let us not think or talk of it now," his mother said in trembling tones. "Let us rejoice in present blessings and be thankful that so many of us are here to enjoy them together. Oh, I thank God every day, Don, that you escaped with life, and though you were so weak and emaciated, were not yet so utterly broken down as so many other poor fellows!"

"And so do I, mother," he responded heartily.

The subject was dropped for the time but was renewed again some hours later by a remark from Dr. Landreth.

"By the way, Don, I saw a statement the other day to the effect that, on the 26th of September last, the Andersonville prisoners passed resolutions asserting that they were as well treated as the Confederate troops. Do you know of any such action on their part? You were one of them at that time."

"Not one of those who passed those resolutions!" returned Don most emphatically. "It was done by prisoners who had accepted employment from the

Rebels, and by no others. They were bad men who had enlisted from other than patriotic motives or had been drafted into the Federal army, and who, if they get their deserts, will be brought to trial by court martial for maltreatment and murder of their fellows when the war is over. I saw one of them kill a comrade just for trying to to climb into a wagon to get a piece of bread.

"Some weeks before the passing of those resolutions, the Rebel adjutant and sergeant came to me with the compliments of the commander of the post and orders to report at once at headquarters, where I was wanted to act as clerk. And if I accepted that position, I was to be furnished with a new suit of gray and plenty to eat and drink—in short, to be treated as one of their officers."

"Wasn't it a temptation?" queried the doctor with a look of sympathy and admiration.

"Yes," replied Don, "I admit that it was, for I was nearly naked and starving. Yet my whole soul revolted at the thought of forsaking the cause of the Union and espousing that of the rebellion. So I unhesitatingly declined the offer.

"Then they told me I would starve to death where I was. I said,

"'It looks very probable, but God is as able to rescue me from this horrible place as he was to take Jonah out of the whale's belly, rescue Daniel from the lions' den, or deliver the Hebrew children from the fiery furnace that Nebuchadnezzar had "heated seven times more than it was wont to be heated."

"'But if it should be His will to let me perish here, then I will die as a Christian man should,—in the path of duty to my God and my country.'"

"Oh, Don," cried Mildred, "I am proud of you, and of all my boys!"

"Mother, do you call uncle Don one of your boys?" asked little Fan in wide-eyed surprise.

"Yes, dear. When he and your uncle Cyril were little fellows, younger than you are now, and I was their big sister, I used to call them my boys."

"Yes," Don said, smiling, "and we often called ourselves so."

"When were you put into that dreadful prison, uncle?" asked Stuart.

"Early in August. I was there when a very strange thing happened.

"There were thirty-three thousand men there, all nearly dying of thirst. Oh, so thirsty were we that I believe any man among us would have given all he had for one drink of clear, cold water! And I assure you that I, for one, was crying to God for help. I had been doing so continually from the time I entered, when, on the tenth day of the month, a large spring of clear, cold water came spontaneously and unexpectedly out of the bank near the dead line.

"I cannot tell you how glad and thankful I was, and I suppose there were few, if any, who did not share my feelings. I am certain that there was no one who did not rejoice.

"But I must tell you of another signal interposition of Providence, without which everyone in that horrible enclosure would, I verily believe, have quickly perished.

"It was in the latter part of August, the heat was intense, the stench from the mortified limbs and bodies of the dead and dying, awful! The air was poisoned by it, so that we were breathing death with every act of respiration.

"Suddenly, a dark cloud gathered right over us, while the horizon all around was perfectly clear. It thundered and lightened, and the rain poured down upon us in torrents.

"That storm wrought our deliverance from immediate death, as it seemed to me, for no words can describe the difference that it made in our horrible prison pen! I am satisfied that, but for that kind interposition of Providence, you would, none of you, ever have seen my face on earth again."

"'Oh, that men would praise the Lord for His goodness and for his wonderful works to the children of men!'" exclaimed Mrs. Keith, gazing with loving, tearful eyes at the son so mercifully preserved from a horrible fate.

"I certainly have great reason to do so, mother," said Don with feeling.

"Oh, uncle, I do hope you will never, never get into that dreadful place again!" cried little Fan.

"I hope not, indeed, my child," he said, "and I do not suppose there is much danger of it, for the war is surely drawing to a close, and I shall not be fit for service for a long time."

The others agreed with him in that opinion as they gazed at him through tear dimmed eyes, for he was but the shadow of his former self.

# CHAPTER XVIII

It was Sunday evening, April 9, 1865. Mildred had remained at home with Fan, who was not quite well, but the rest of the family were at church.

The news of the past week had been so favorable to the Union cause that all loyal hearts beat high with hope that peace was near at hand—peace, with a saved country.

Richmond had been captured six days before, and it was known that Grant was in hot pursuit of Lee.

Mildred's thoughts were full of it as she sat there—to all intents and purposes alone, for Fan had fallen asleep on the sofa—full of the momentous crisis to the country and the possible peril of son, brothers, nephew.

Ah, who should say that one or more, or all, were not even now in the agonies of death by shot, shell, sword, or bayonet!

She rose and paced the floor, wrestling in prayer for them all but especially her beloved first-born son, beseeching that if God's will were so, he might return to her in safety and health.

The front door opened, quick steps came through the hall, and Stuart and Marcia rushed in, breathless with excitement and joy.

"Mother, mother!" they cried., "The war is over! Lee has surrendered! It was given out in church. A man came hurrying in and handed a telegram to the minister just as he was going to pronounce the benediction. He read it out. It said that Lee had surrendered to Grant; and everybody seemed nearly wild with joy and just burst into singing *The Doxology*, 'Praise God from whom all blessings flow,' as if they all thought of it at the same instant.

"Oh, mother, it was glorious! And isn't it glorious news?"

"It is, indeed! The Union saved! The war over! Oh, thank God! Thank God!" she cried, weeping for joy and gratitude.

Dr. Landreth came in at that moment. Professional duties had unavoidably detained him from attendance upon the evening service, but he had heard the glad tidings on the street.

"Milly, my love, my darling, you have heard?" he said in half-tremulous accents as she flew into his outstretched arms.

"Yes," she sobbed, dropping her head upon his shoulder. "Oh, praise God for His goodness! Now, if we only knew of the safety of our boy and the others!"

"They are in the hands of that God whose goodness and mercy we are adoring," he said with feeling, "and I trust that we shall soon hear that all is well with them."

"What are you all crying about?" asked Fan, rousing from her sleep. "Oh, I hope it isn't that Percy's killed?"

"No, no, it's good news," Marcia hastened to reply. "Lee has surrendered, and the war is over."

"Father," she said, turning to him as with a sudden thought, "is there sure to be no more fighting?"

"No," he said, "there are other armies to surrender, but it is altogether likely they will do so as soon as they hear of Lee's action because there is plainly now no hope at all of the success of the rebellion — their capital being taken and their principal army scattered, while their resources must be pretty completely exhausted."

"And will Percy come home tomorrow?" asked Fan with a look of eager delight.

"No, my child, things can't be done quite so fast as that," her father answered. "But I think we may hope to see him in a few weeks."

And now Zillah and her daughter came in, their hearts so full of joy and gratitude that they could not refrain from seeking an exchange of sympathy with the dear ones, who, they could not doubt, were in much the same frame of mind as themselves.

The sisters wept in each other's arms, mingling smiles and laughter with their sobs and tears, then, calming down somewhat, talked hopefully of the speedy return of their sons and brothers.

"Let us go over to father's," proposed Zillah presently. "I don't think I can sleep till I have seen him and mother."

"Agreed!" said the doctor, catching up Fan and wrapping a shawl round her. "I'll carry the baby," he added laughingly. "It won't hurt her. And Milly, you may follow with the other two."

They met Cyril's wife and Annis halfway, but they turned about and accompanied the larger party to Mr. Keith's.

A half-hour was spent in rejoicing together, exchanging congratulations, singing *The Doxology*,

and offering up thanks to the Giver of all good—
first Mr. Keith and then the doctor leading in
prayer.

After that, they separated with glad good nights.

"Father," said Stuart, as they entered their own
door, "I want to put out all our flags as soon as it's
light enough to see. May I?"

"Certainly," was the ready reply, "and I think we
should have an illumination at night in honor of the
return of peace."

"Yes," said Mildred, "though we don't want to
exult over our fallen foe. I hardly feel that they are
enemies any longer. They are our own people, and
now that they have given up and the Union is safe,
we'll do all we can to help them to recuperate from
their losses. At least, that is my desire, and I do
believe the feeling is general over all the North."

"I think it is, with rare exceptions," assented the
doctor.

A few days of joyous excitement, and then—that
awful blow that struck the nation down from the
heights of glad exultation to the depths of woe—
the base and cowardly assassination which robbed
her of him who had stood at the helm of the ship of
state while she was tossing about among those
fearful breakers and, with the help of God, had
guided her safely through them into comparatively
calm and peaceful waters.

At early dawn on Saturday morning, Dr.
Landreth was called from his bed to visit a patient.

Mildred was attending to her morning preparations when she heard his returning footsteps. They
were not as light and elastic as they had been since
the news of the surrender, and noting the change,
she said to herself:

"Something is wrong. I fear poor Mr. Dale is dead or dying, and it is so dreadful to Charlie to lose a patient."

The next moment he entered the room.

She turned toward him to speak a word of sympathy and comfort, but catching sight of his face, she read in it such grief, horror, and despair that she staggered and would have fallen had he not caught her in his arms.

"Percy?" she gasped.

"It is not that, love," he faltered. "I have no news from our boy or your brothers. But—Lincoln—has been assassinated, Seward, too, it is said, and perhaps Grant."

Releasing her, he dropped into a chair, bowed his head upon his breast, and sobbed aloud, while she stood speechless with grief, the tears streaming over her cheeks.

"It is the worst thing which could possibly have happened for my native section," he said. "The South had no better friend, and the noblest, kindest heart that ever beat in human breast is stilled forever by the base and cowardly blow of an assassin."

Then were there weeping and lamentation all over the land, and everywhere the signs of joy were exchanged for those of mourning. The people mourned their friend and benefactor, the nation its chief.

But the Union was saved, the war substantially over. In a few weeks all the armies of the Confederacy had surrendered and disbanded. The Union forces were disbanded also, and the soldiers returned to their homes.

The day that brought back their "boys in blue"

was a glad one indeed to our friends in Pleasant Plains.

Mildred and Zillah could scarcely recognize their fair stripling sons in the bronzed young men that claimed to be the same yet looked so different.

Yet there was no room for complaint of lack of warmth in the reception given them. Their mothers welcomed them with a joy too deep for anything but tears.

They had come back unharmed physically, and after a long, searching gaze into her boy's face, Mildred drew a sigh of thankfulness—convinced that her prayer that he might return to her as pure as he went had been granted.

Harry Duncan came with the others, his principal errand to hunt up his old aunt and carry her home again.

It was an errand that would have spoiled his welcome, if anything could, for all were loathe to part with the dear lady who had been as a mother to Mrs. Stuart Keith and a grandmother to her descendants.

But she had her own home in Lansdale and felt that her place was there, so she made arrangements to return with Harry at the expiration of a week from the time of his arrival. He could not be persuaded to remain longer than that, being on the eve of marriage with May Allison, a sister of Horace Dinsmore's wife, and anxious to get into business so that he might be able to make a comfortable support for himself and her.

There was a good opening for him in Lansdale. His prospects were bright, and being naturally of a lively, hopeful disposition, he was the life of the company while he remained.

But, indeed, all were jubilant, for was not the war over, the Union saved? And the dear ones who had risked everything for its salvation — were they not restored to their homes and parents, wives and children, sound in health and limb, apparently none the worse for all the hardships they had endured?

Their arrival was something of a surprise. They were expected by the evening train, and grand preparations were afoot for their reception.

Marcia, Stuart, and Fan were permitted to stay at home from school and help their mother with hers. They were anxious to have Percy find everything in the best possible order, indoors and out. They had talked it all over, again and again, since the close of the war had given them the hope of his speedy return.

The horses and the garden were Stuart's special care. Percy must find the former sleek and fat, the latter free from weeds and as neat and orderly as hands could make it.

It was nearly that now, but Stuart perceived some need of improvement and was busy there, Jim assisting him, while Mildred and her daughters took equal pains within doors, especially with the arrangement and adornment of Percy's own room.

Glad tears glistened in the mother's eyes, and her heart swelled with grateful emotion as she went about her pleasant task, returning to it again and again to put loving, lingering touches here and there.

At last she could find nothing more to do there, or in any other of the apartments except the kitchen, where she repaired to make Percy's favorite cake. Marcia and Fan assisted at their own earnest request, for was it not the greatest of pleasures to do anything for the enjoyment of the dear, long-absent brother?

It was charming summer weather, and doors and windows stood wide open. They heard the whistle of the locomotive and the distant rush and roar of the incoming train but only with the thought that the next arrival would bring their returning wanderers. And so they went on with their labors, Mildred rather silent, the two girls chattering joyously.

But presently there was a sound of wheels in the road before the house, then of footsteps coming up the gravel walk and onto the porch.

"Father's come home," remarked Fan. "I hope he won't have to go to the country again before—"

But her sentence was left unfinished, for a tall form filled the doorway leading to the sitting room, and, with a cry, her mother dropped the spoon with which she was stirring her cake and sprang into the arms opened to receive her.

"Percy! My son, my son!" she sobbed, as he held her close, kissing lips and cheek and brow. "Thank God! Thank God that my boy is restored to me!"

Dr. Landreth stood behind his son, watching the little scene with tear-dimmed eyes.

He had driven to the depot as the train came in, impressed with the thought that there was a possibility of the returning soldiers coming a little earlier than was expected. And glad he was that he had done so, for the instant the train stopped, they were seen hurrying out from it, their bronzed faces lighted up with the joy of finding themselves again at home.

When the first breathless surprise and the first half-frantic embraces were over, and something like calmness had been restored, the young people began to note the changes in each other's appearance.

"Percy, how you have altered! I should hardly have known you!" exclaimed Marcia, gazing on him with fond, admiring eyes.

"How?" he asked, looking smilingly at her. "Do you perceive anything more than that I have acquired a few coats of tan?"

"Oh, yes, a great deal more! You have grown taller, broader, and—so manly. You went away a boy, and it seems to me you have come back a man, even if you are scarcely more than eighteen."

"Thank you," he returned merrily and with a pleased look. "But it seems to me that you and Stuart and Fan have changed quite as much as I, though you have stayed at home. You have all three grown very much, and you, Mar, I notice, are as tall as mother now and look quite like a young lady. I shall be proud to gallant you about and introduce you to strangers as my sister."

They had withdrawn into the sitting room, Mildred and the girls forgetting all about their unfinished work.

And Rachel was quite as oblivious of domestic cares and duties, for she, too, was rejoicing over her lost and found. Sam had come back with Captain Ormsby and reached Dr. Landreth's house some five minutes after Percy's arrival.

It was the staid, practical Stuart who came to the rescue.

"Mother," he said, "I saw, just before Percy came, that you and the girls were making a cake.

May I try to finish it for you? I've often watched how you did it."

"That is a kind offer, my boy," she returned, smiling affectionately upon him, "especially as it would be an act of self-denial on your part, to leave the rest of us just now. But I think a better plan will be for you all to come to the kitchen with me. Then we can go on with our talk while I finish my work myself."

"I approve of that plan," laughed the doctor, leading the way. "The kitchen of this house, with the wife and mother in it, is to my thinking quite as attractive as any other of its rooms."

"Yes, sir," said Percy, "and I have often wished myself in it again, thinking of the pleasant talks mother and I have had together there while I have helped her with the work when she had no girl."

"And I daresay you have found use for the knowledge and skill so attained."

"Oh, yes, sir! There have been times when I was glad enough to be able to cook a meal for myself and comrades," replied Percy.

Mildred asked for her brothers and nephew and was told that they, too, had arrived safely and in health. Then Percy went on to tell of some of his experiences and adventures while in the army, all proving very interesting to this hearers.

But the cake was scarcely in the oven when Rupert, Cyril, and Wallace and his wife and children came in, the returned soldiers anxious to see and greet these loved ones as they had already greeted the others still nearer and dearer.

Usually, the domestic machinery of Mildred's household moved with the precision of clock work, but today, dinner was delayed by at least half an hour, for who could think of such sublunary matters as meals, with all this delicious excitement going on?

Mildred and Rachel did so, finally, and when the board was spread, it was a tempting one to behold. Most of the party were ready to do it justice, though the mother could scarcely eat for gazing at her long-absent son, whom she was rejoicing over almost as one restored from the dead, and listening to the sound of his voice, which was as sweetest music to her ears.

A few days were given up almost entirely to the pleasure of the reunion, then they began to consider the business of life again.

The doctor was greatly pleased that Percy himself broached the subject of his future, as regarded the employment of time and talent.

"Father," he asked, "are you and mother still in favor of my taking a college course?"

"We would be glad to have you do so," the doctor replied. "It will not unfit you for anything you may wish to undertake afterward, and should you choose a profession, it will be a very great advantage. Have you any idea what you would prefer as your lifework?"

"Yes, sir," answered the lad promptly. "It is my desire to follow the example of my grandfather Keith."

"Become a lawyer?"

"Yes, sir. My next choice would be your profession, but I think I may be better fitted for the law."

"Well, my boy, if you have a decided preference for any one business or profession, I wish you to follow that, because a man is always more likely to succeed in employment that is to his taste.

"But whether your choice be law, medicine, or something else, I trust that your desire and purpose will be to serve God to the utmost of your ability in the performance of its duties."

"Yes, father, and do you not think I may serve him in the practice of the law?"

"Certainly, my son. Good, conscientious, Christian men are needed in that profession as well as everywhere else. They are needed to see justice done to both the innocent and the guilty. They have often opportunity to frustrate the evil designs of wicked, unscrupulous men and to rescue the helpless and oppressed from those who would rob or otherwise maltreat them."

"I am glad you are satisfied with my choice, father," Percy said, then wen on:

"I have lost a year but am far from grudging it to my country. Indeed, Cousin Stuart and I both feel that we are very fortunate to have escaped without the loss of health or limb.

"Of course, we have grown rusty in our studies, and we propose to review them this summer and be ready for college in the fall. Then we both intend to study law after we have graduated from college, and when we are ready for practice, to go into business together."

"You seem to have your plans already cut and dried," remarked his father, smiling.

"Oh, yes, sir, we have talked it all over a good many times."

"Well, I am glad, very glad, to learn that you are planning to go to work at once, for I have felt a little apprehensive that army life might have destroyed your taste for steady industry, and I could only hope that a sense of duty and accountability to God would enable you to resume it in spite of disinclination."

"I'm afraid we may find it a little difficult at first to settle down to steady work," Percy said. "But what's a man worth, father, if he can't control his inclination and make himself do what he knows he ought?"

The doctor grasped his son's hand and shook it heartily, exclaiming, "My boy, I am proud of you! You owe very much to your mother's counsels and instruction."

"To yours, also, father," Percy returned with a look of filial gratitude and affection.

Mildred's heart throbbed with motherly pride and pleasure when her husband repeated this conversation to her, adding, "My dearest, it is, I am sure, largely owing to your faithful training that our son is turning out so noble a fellow. I think he is, and will continue to be, a credit and comfort to us and a blessing to the land of his birth. You have done, you are doing, well for your country in raising up for her patriotic and God-fearing citizens, men and women," he added smilingly, "for the others give promise of equalling their elder brother in sterling qualities of heart and mind."

"They are dear children, all of them," returned Mildred with emotion. "We have tried to train them aright,—both you and I—and to set a good example before them, asking wisdom and help of God. And I believe He is fulfilling to us His gracious promise, 'Train up a child in the way he should go: and when he is old, he will not depart from it.' To Him be all the glory of any success we have had or may have in the future."

# CHAPTER XIX

"Ah, who is that? Somebody for me, I suppose," said Dr. Landreth as a horseman came galloping up the street and drew rein before the gate.

"The doctor!" he shouted. "Is the doctor in?"

"Yes," answered Percy, who was seated on the porch, where his father had left him a few moments before.

"Yes," answered the doctor himself, as he hurried out from the open door. "What is wanted?"

"You, doctor. Sam Smith's wife horribly burned. I'm afraid she'll die afore you get there. It's a good two miles, you know, out in the country."

"Yes, I'll not delay a moment. Percy—" he said, turning toward the spot where the young man had stood. But Percy was already off to the stable for a horse, which he saddled and bridled with all speed while the doctor got his remedies together.

"Thank you, my son. I see you are your old thoughtful self," he said as he mounted in haste. And with the last word, he was away like the wind.

Percy stood on the porch looking after him till he was out of sight, then, turning, found his mother close at this side.

"Mother," he said, "what a useful man my father is! I'm not sure that the medical profession is not the most useful of all."

"But you don't think of going into it?"

"Would you wish me to, mother?" he asked.

"No," she said, "certainly not, if it is not your preference. I think, that, other things being equal, we can always do best what we like to do. Your father has just been repeating to me the talk you and he had on the subject, and I am well satisfied with your choice, for I believe you may serve God as acceptably in the one profession as in the other.

"And I am very glad indeed," she went on, "that you are not disposed to idleness but are ready to take up at once old duties and your interrupted preparation for your lifework."

Just then Miss Stanhope was seen approaching the gate.

Percy hurried down the path to open it for her.

"Thank you, dear boy," she said with her cheery smile. "You are a gallant gentleman, like your father and grandfather before you."

"I consider that a very high compliment, Aunt Wealthy," he answered. "My father and grandfather are my models."

"Sit down, auntie," Mildred said, drawing forward a comfortable arm chair. "Your presence is always welcome."

"Thank you. But I'll only sit while you get your bonnet on, for you want me to go shopping with you."

"No, I wasn't thinking of it. I believe I have none to do at present," returned Mildred, looking a little surprised.

"There!" exclaimed the old lady. "I suppose I've put things fore end wrongmost, as I generally do. I want to get some little gifts for the children!"

"Oh, yes," said Mildred. "I'll go with you willingly. I'll be ready in a moment. Percy, entertain your aunt till I come back." And she hurried away as she spoke.

Aunt Wealthy turned smilingly to him.

"How well I remember when you were no older than your mother is. And she was a sweet girl! Quite the ring of the town, I always thought , for she had plenty of beaux, and though she wasn't one to boast of her conquests, I'm pretty sure she had half a dozen offers or more."

"I don't doubt it, if the young men had good taste," said Percy, "though I can hardly think she could even have been any sweeter or more beautiful than she is now."

"Now, auntie, I am ready and at your service," Mildred said, stepping from the open doorway with her bonnet on.

The old lady rose with alacrity. "You are a good girl, Milly. You never keep one waiting. We'll go at once, so as to have plenty of time, for I want to look over the remnants, see all they have, and choose the prettiest."

"I hardly think you will find many large enough to be of much use, auntie," Mildred said as they passed out of the gate, Percy holding it open for them. "The children are getting so grown up, and dress patterns have to be so large nowadays."

"Cyril's children are small yet," returned Miss Stanhope.

"But they wear nothing but white."

"Oh, well, I've always found remnants come in

useful for something! I can piece some quilts for May—Harry's wife that is to be."

"Dear auntie, you are always thinking of others and working for them," returned Mildred with an affectionate look into the kindly old face. "But I am sure it is not worthwhile for you to wear yourself out piecing quilts."

"Pooh, child! It will be a pleasure," was the good-humored rejoinder. "Do you know I feel quite lost with no soldiers' stockings to knit, no shirts to make for the poor fellows. Really, there's nothing to do for any of them except Harry, and he's getting a wife to look after him and his clothes."

"Don't worry, auntie dear, you'll soon find plenty of objects upon which to expend your money and your labors. There must be a great number of soldiers' widows and orphans left destitute, or nearly so."

"There! That's just the work for me to go at!" exclaimed Miss Stanhope delightedly. "And there'll be plenty of the orphans small enough to work up for the remnants! Why, it's just the thing, Milly! I'm so glad you turned my attention to it!"

And, full of pleased excitement, the old lady hurried on and into the first store they came to, where she asked, half breathlessly, to be immediately shown all the remnants of dress goods the establishment had on hand and was eagerly bought them all.

Mildred thought she would find her money thrown away on some of them, but it was quite useless to try to check her.

The same thing was repeated in several other stores, and gifts were purchased for all the children in the family connection. Aunt Wealthy gathered up the last of her parcels, stowing them in a handbag which she carried, and they started for the door.

"Madam, you have got my purse in your bag! Please hand it out to me," exclaimed an angry voice behind them.

Much astonished, they turned quickly toward the speaker.

She was a stout, middle-aged, rather coarse-looking woman, a stranger to them both, her face red and eyes flashing with anger.

"Give up my purse," she cried again, seizing Miss Stanhope by the wrist. "Give it up, I say, or I'll have you arrested."

"I know nothing about your purse, Madam," returned the old lady in a gentle tone but beginning to tremble with nervous excitement.

"You needn't tell me that," said her accuser. "It's in your bag this minute! I saw you put it in."

"You are surely mistaken," said Mildred.

"You certainly are, as I will soon show you, if you will let go of my wrist," said aunt Wealthy. And as the woman released her, she opened the bag, and pulled out — not her own purse but, to her utter amazement and confusion, that which she was accused of having taken.

Without a word she handed it to the claimant and walked out of the store. She was trembling so that Mildred had to put an arm round her to keep her from falling.

"Oh, Milly, Milly!" she half sobbed, "everybody will think I'm a thief!"

"No, no, dear auntie, no one will, unless it is that rude woman. She must be a stranger to this part of the country, but everybody who lives in the town knows you and your absent-mindedness. How was it, do you think, that the purse got into your bag?"

"I must have gathered it up with my parcels, taking it for my own. Dear me, I'm afraid I'm hardly fit to be at large!" she added, laughing hysterically.

It was a relief to Mildred that, at that moment, Harry Duncan joined them and gave Miss Stanhope the support of his arm.

He asked the cause of her agitation, heard the story, called it a good joke, and tried to laugh away her chagrin and her fears.

Left alone by his mother and aunt, Percy walked over to his grandfather's. Celestia Ann was tying up some roses in the front yard and accosted him as he entered.

"Glad to see you, Percy. I hain't hardly had no chance to speak to you sence you come home."

"No," he said, grasping warmly the toil-hardened hand she held out to him, "it's been a whirl of excitement since we got back. But I'm very glad to see you looking so well, Celestia Ann."

"Yes, I'm all right, but those nephews o' mine that 'listed as privateers—one on 'em was killed outright, and t'other pretty nigh starved to death at Andersonville," she said, the big tears rolling fast down her cheeks.

"Is that so?" cried Percy. "Oh, Celestia Ann, I'm very sorry to hear it!"

"Yes," she said, "and old folks is heartbroke, and so'm I for that matter. I hope the people o' this country'll never forgit t' appreciate the herculaneum efforts the boys in blue made to save the Union, or what their folks has had to bear in givin' 'em up to do the work o' puttin' down the rebellion."

"No, indeed, I trust not," said Percy.

"And I hope we'll never have another war," she went on. "It's my 'pinion that this one ort to be considered big enough to do for as long as we are a nation, though I ain't sorry they fit it out, 'cause it's plain as day we wouldn't never have had no peace nor comfort if they hadn't.

"But that 'sassinatin' o' the President was 'most the wust of all. Why, when I heered the news, it 'peared like pins and needles—millions of 'em—went right through my system."

"It was terrible, and about the most disastrous thing for the South that could have happened," said Percy sadly.

"What was, cousin Percy?" asked little Marcia Keith, his uncle Cyril's daughter, coming up to them with a pet cat in her arms.

"President Lincoln's death," he answered.

"Oh, Marcia, do put that cat down!" exclaimed Celestia Ann. "I can't bear to see you a holdin' it up so near your face. When we was little, our mother wouldn't never let us play with cats, for fear we get one o' their hairs in our stomachs and die of consumption."

"Oh, I'm not afraid, and my mother never cares," replied the little girl, tripping back to the house, still holding fast to her pet.

"Don't you think she's doin' a dangerous thing, Percy?" asked Celestia Ann, sending an anxious glance after the child.

"My father would be the better person to consult about the matter," he answered, turning away to hide the twinkle of fun in his eye.

"Well, I've a good mind to speak to the doctor about it the very next time I get a chance," she said, returning to her work while Percy moved on toward the house.

His grandfather, grandmother, and aunts were sitting on the porch. He joined them and was still there when his mother and aunt Wealthy returned from their shopping, Harry Duncan accompanying them.

"Oh, auntie dear, your walk seems to have tired you out!" exclaimed Mrs. Keith in accents of concern as the old lady sank exhausted into the easy chair immediately brought forward for her. "You should not have attempted so much at once."

"No, no, Marcia, it isn't that," panted Miss Stanhope, "but something unpleasant that—that happened. Mildred shall tell you the story. Dear, dear, what am I coming to! The older I live, and the longer I grow, the more topsy-turvy and absent-minded I get."

"But you never grew very long, and you don't grow any longer, auntie," said Harry, half tenderly, half laughingly, as he took a seat by her side and began to fan her flushed and heated face.

"No, there's not much of me but quite enough such as it is," she said, laughing her little hysterical laugh. "Now, Milly, tell them the story."

"It was nothing of any consequence, except as it distressed and troubled you, auntie dear," Mildred said.

Then, addressing the others, she said, "It was only that, in collecting her parcels, she unconsciously gathered up with them another woman's purse and put it into her bag. And then the woman—being a stranger to aunt Wealthy and not understanding the thing — demanded her property in a very rude and insulting way."

"Oh, aunt Wealthy, that is not anything to be distressed about," several of them said, speaking together.

"No, you mustn't mind it at all. It is all right now," said Harry.

"And we're all ready and anxious to see the remnants," he added mischievously.

"How did you know there were any?" she asked, looking a little surprised.

"Because, my best and dearest of aunts, I know you of old," he returned with an affectionate, laughing look into her face.

"Here comes father at last," remarked Percy. "He has been gone a long while. I wonder how that poor woman is."

"What woman?" asked his grandmother.

"He was called to a Mrs. Smith living in the country somewhere," Percy answered. "And the messenger said she was so horribly burned that he feared she would die."

Dismounting at his own gate, the doctor gave his horse into Jim's charge, then walked over to the house of his father-in-law.

"The woman is dead," Mildred said as he came up the path to the porch where they were sitting.

"Why, how do you know?" asked Annis.

"By the way Charlie looks and walks, his air of depression. The loss of a patient is very dreadful to him."

In answer to the sympathizing, inquiring look his wife bestowed upon him as he stepped into their midst, the doctor said, "Yes, she is gone. It was a very sad affair. She and her husband had been into town with their marketing and were on their way home again, he smoking a pipe, when all at once, they discovered that her cotton dress was in a blaze.

"There was quite a breeze blowing, and in an instant she was enveloped in flames. They both made every effort to put out the fire, he says, but did not succeed till she was so badly burned that there was no possibility of saving her life."

"Oh, dreadful! But how did she take fire?" asked Annis.

"From his pipe; there was no other way. Boys," he said, turning to his sons and Stuart Ormsby, for by this time they were all there, "take warning, and don't smoke."

"I promise you I'll not under such circumstances," said Harry. "Not when there can be the slightest danger of my wife taking fire from my pipe or cigar."

"I should think Sam Smith would eschew tobacco for the rest of his life, if he has any heart or conscience," remarked Annis rather severely. "Does he care, Charlie?"

"Care? He's almost distracted, says he'll never smoke again. But I doubt if he keeps his resolution, having been wedded to the habit for many years. He's an elderly man and began when he was a mere lad, he tells me."

"I hear you are going into the mercantile business," remarked old Mr. Keith, turning to Harry.

"Yes, sir, that's my intention. You see, a certain dear, little old lady who has been more than a mother to me is very fond of remnants—of dress goods and the like—and if I'm in that line, I can perhaps put her in the way of getting all she wants.

"I think of managing my buying and selling so that there'll always be a yard or two left over from every piece of goods, so that she'll be sure to lead the happiest of lives, busy as a bee from morning to night, cutting out and making garments for any poor child she can find in need of one."

"Ah, Harry! How you enjoy making sport of your foolish old auntie," Miss Stanhope said, looking up into his face with a good-humored smile. "Well, if she's to go on making such blunders as that of today, perhaps she may need a lawyer friend more than a merchant."

"I think she has several of them already," remarked Mr. Keith. "Wallace Ormsby and I will always be at your service, Aunt Wealthy. But I am not apprehensive that you are likely to have occasion to call upon us."

"Beside, Percy and I hope, some of these days, to constitute a young firm that will be quite as ready to attend to anything for you, Aunt Wealthy," said Stuart Ormsby.

"Thank you," she said. "I see there's no occasion for Harry to give up the mercantile business, at least not to undertake the law on my account."

"So you think of following your grandfather's profession, boys?" Mr. Keith said with a pleased look at Stuart and Percy, who were standing together.

"Well, I like the idea of another Keith and Ormsby as successors to the present firm. But may it be many years, Wallace, before you have to give place to them. However, Ormsby, Keith, & Ormsby would sound very well."

"Yes, sir, so it would," replied Wallace, "but it will be some years yet before the boys are ready for practice, and I am in no hurry to take the place of senior partner. I think it is time you were relieved from labor, but I should be sorry indeed to lose the benefit of your advice in difficult cases. Your extensive knowledge of law and your many years of experience make you a far more valuable partner than either of these lads can hope to become before he reaches middle age."

# CHAPTER XX

PERCY WAS INCLINED to take up again his old home duties and responsibilities, but his brother objected.

"No, Percy, dear old fellow," he said, "there isn't more than I can attend to with perfect ease. And you—the chap who has been fighting for his country—ought to have all your time to catch up in your studies."

"You're very good, Stuart," returned Percy, "but I must have exercise or I shall lose my health."

"Yes, of course, but you can take enough of that playing ball, riding, driving, and boating on the river. You ought to have all the fun you possibly can, after your hard times in the army."

"What a good fellow you are, Stuart!" said Percy. "There isn't a lazy bone in your body."

"I hope not. Perhaps it might do for me to be a trifle lazy once in a while, if I were as smart as my older brother. But as I'm not, I'll have to try to make up for my dullness by steady industry."

"That dullness lies wholly in your imagination, old fellow," returned Percy affectionately. "You may be a little slower than I am, but it won't surprise me if you turn out worth two of me in the end."

"Well, I shall be greatly astonished if I do. But you stick to your books now this summer and get well ready for college by fall, and I'll see to whatever father and mother would have their sons attend to about the house and grounds. There isn't much, now that we have both Sam and Jim, not to speak of Rachel."

"All right," returned Percy, "but I'll want your company in all my sports — Mar's too, when it's riding, driving, or boating. What a pretty, ladylike girl she is, Stuart! I believe she's just going to be mother over again."

"Yes, she's as good as gold and as handsome, too. I'm proud of her."

The boys were on the porch, and Mildred, in the sitting room looking out upon it, happened to overhear this talk. It pleased her, as did some things told her by Stuart Ormsby an hour later.

He came in, asking for Percy, but on learning that he was out, sat down for a chat with his aunt and Marcia.

Naturally, the talk turned upon the life the lads had led during the past year.

"Percy was very popular in the regiment," remarked Stuart. "And no wonder, for he was always on the lookout to do somebody a kindness. I've known him to take a tired fellow's watch when he was nearly as tired himself or had a bad headache.

"And after a battle, he was sure to be doing something for the wounded, if it was only to carry them a drink of water or offer a prayer for them or tell them the way to heaven. I've listened to him sometimes and thought he made it quite as clear and plain as the chaplain could.

"Then he had learned from uncle how to bandage a limb, and he often helped the surgeons at that."

"I am very glad to hear that he was so useful," Mildred said, her eyes shining with pleasure. "And I suspect you must have shared his labors, to know so much about them."

"Well, yes, some of them I did, Aunt Mildred," said Stuart modestly, a slight blush mantling his cheek. "I tried to follow his good example, but I couldn't talk to the poor fellows like he did, or pray with them. I've told him sometimes that I was half inclined to think he ought to be a minister, but I'm glad he chooses the law because we can be together."

"I am quite satisfied with his choice," Mildred said, "though I should have rejoiced to see him in the ministry."

"Perhaps Stuart will choose that profession."

"No," spoke up Marcia, "Stuart says he's quite resolved to be a doctor. He wants to help father, and, besides, thinks he should greatly enjoy relieving sick and wounded people of their sufferings."

"Just like my noble boy!" the mother exclaimed. "Since he was old enough to talk, he has always wanted to help and comfort others, especially his father and mother."

"Is the doctor in?" asked a familiar voice at the open door.

"No, Celestia Ann, not now, though I think he will be presently," Mildred answered. "Is anybody sick at father's?"

"No, Miss Mildred, the folks there is all 'bout as usual. But I ain't been feelin' so real well myself these last several days."

"Haven't you?" returned Mildred. "I am sorry to hear it. How is it that you are suffering?"

"Oh, I ain't got no appetite to eat, and my stomach feels qualmish-like, and my head takes to kind o' spinning round. And I'm afeared I'm goin' to have a bilious detack or digestion of the brain—one or t'other or something else. I'd like to see the doctor and git somethin' to take afore I git any worse."

"There, he's just going into his office," said Marcia, glancing from the window. "You'd better hurry in there, before he goes away again, Celestia Ann."

"So I will," she said, hastening from the room.

"I hope uncle is skillful in warding off bilious detacks, and digestion of the brain," laughed Stuart.

"As capable in that line as any other doctor, I presume," returned Marcia with a mirthful look. "But we mustn't laugh at Celestia Ann, for she's always been very good to us. Hasn't she, Stuart?"

"Yes, so she has," he acknowledged. "And I suppose if she had had the same opportunities that we have enjoyed, she would have spoken quite as correctly."

He drew out his watch and, glancing at it, said, "I must be going. I have an errand to do for mother before dinner."

He came in again after tea that evening. He and Percy had been constantly together in their campaigns and were now so strongly attached that they were seldom seen apart. And as neither family liked to be separated from the returned son and brother, and all were fond of each other's society, the consequence was that their evenings were apt to be spent all together, now in one house and in the other, the grandfather's being as often chosen as either Dr. Landreth's or Mr. Ormsby's.

Cyril had taken his wife and children away to a home of their own. Harry Duncan was gone, and aunt Wealthy with him, but they still had four returned soldiers among them who could sometimes be induced to fight their battles over again or relate interesting incidents connected with the struggle which had come under their own observation.

Percy and his cousin had taken up their studies as proposed, and they pursued them diligently all summer. They had been well advanced in them at the time of enlisting in the army, and when the time for entering college came, they were ready for the sophomore class.

Before that, however, they had an adventure that came near terminating very sadly. It was in the height of summer, the heat exceedingly oppressive.

"Father," Percy said as they sat about the dinner table, "we boys are talking of taking a moonlight row on the river this evening, if you and mother are willing."

"Very well," returned the doctor, "I see no objection. But what do you say, wife?"

"If you think it quite safe, my dear, I give my consent," she answered a little doubtfully.

"I'll not go if it is to cause you anxiety, mother," Percy hastened to say, "but if it won't, I'm sure we would all enjoy it very much. We want to take our sisters and would be delighted to have our mothers along also."

"Thank you, my son," she said, "but that would give you too heavy a boatload and increase the danger, if there is any."

"Oh! If you will all go, we'll borrow a boat and have two."

"Whose?" asked his father.

"Tom Clark's."

"No, you mustn't take it. I don't think it's in safe condition," returned the doctor.

"Then we will not, sir, of course," said Percy. "But you are willing we should go in our own?"

"Yes, with a proper load. It was not intended to hold more than six."

"Then, mother, I think it would be ever so nice for you and our two aunts to go this time. With the three boys to row you, that would just make the six," said Marcia with a glad, eager, entreating look into her mother's face.

"Oh, yes, mother, do!" cried Fan. "I just know you'd enjoy it."

"Not half so much as my daughters would," responded Mildred with a pleased smile. "And if their father thinks there is no danger, I should rather let them go."

"But, mother, we go so often, and you almost always stay at home."

"I'll go when your father does," she said merrily, smiling across the table at him. "It wasn't easy to say no when we were young and he invited me to go searching for enjoyment with him."

"My dear," he said, returning the smile, "it is high time there was a renewal of those old attentions. Will you take a drive with me this afternoon?"

"Yes, indeed, if you can spare the time," she answered promptly, her eyes shining brightly. "And we will let the boys and girls take their turn boating this evening—if you really consider it to be entirely safe?"

"I see no reason to apprehend danger," he answered. "Three strong lads, used to the river, in a boat that is in perfect condition, and carrying only a proper load—what is there to fear?"

"I suppose really nothing," she said. "But I was just thinking of the very rapid current and the deceitfulness of moonlight, for dangerous places are apt to look safe by it."

"We are all ready to give up the project, if you wish it, mother," Percy repeated.

"No," she said, "I have confidence in your father's judgment and should be sorry to deprive any of you of the pleasure I am sure you will have if you go. It will be cool on the river, and everything looking lovely by the moonlight. You are trusty boys, too," she added with a loving look and smile.

"Thank you, mother. We will try to deserve your confidence," they both replied.

"Has aunt Zillah consented to let Ada go?" asked Marcia.

"I don't know. Stuart has not reported yet on that," replied Percy. "I'm a little afraid she won't, for I think she is more apt to be timid about trusting her children than mother is."

"But Ada's good at coaxing," said Marcia laughingly, "and aunt Zillah is more easily coaxed than our mother is."

"Why, Mar, you know mother never did let us coax," said Fan. "And I believe mother's ways are best," she added with a loving look into Mildred's face.

The look was returned with one quite as affectionate, while the doctor said, "I have always thought your mother a very wise woman."

Ada ran over during the course of the afternoon to announce with glee that, though her mother had at first refused her consent to let her join the boating party, she had succeeded in gaining it by persevering arguments and entreaties, Stuart helping her, and insisting that there could not be any danger.

So they went, starting shortly after sundown, as the moon rose that night with the setting of the sun.

The boys rowed upstream several miles, keeping near the shore to avoid the strong current setting the other way. The air was pleasantly cool on the river, and they moved slowly, enjoying it greatly after the heat of the day, occasionally resting on their oars, laughing, talking, jesting in innocent fashion, and singing songs patriotic, comic, and pathetic, their young voices blending in sweet harmony.

On their return, the boys had no need to exert themselves at the oars. They merely allowed the boat to float with the current, Stuart Ormsby steering.

They grew silent and meditative as they neared home, but no one noticed that Fan had fallen asleep.

The little pier at the foot of Dr. Landreth's garden, whence they had embarked and where they were to land, lay in deep shadow from overhanging trees, and Stuart miscalculating the distance a little in the darkness, the boat struck against it with a sudden jar that sent the sleeping child out into the stream.

All heard the heavy plunge, the frightened cry, saw the white dress float for a single instant on the top of the water, then disappear as its wearer sank to the bottom.

Marcia and Ada shrieked, "It's Fan! It's Fan! She's in the water! Oh, she'll drown!"

But Percy had already jerked off his coat and plunged in after her.

He was a good swimmer, but the moon had gone under a cloud and he could see nothing, and the swift current was difficult to stem.

Fan rose and sank two or three times before he could reach her. He was almost in despair, but sending up an agonized, though silent, cry for help, he tried again, and this time clutched her dress.

In another moment he had laid her on the pier and drawn himself up beside her apparently lifeless form.

He was exhausted and panting, but the two Stuarts instantly caught up Fan and bore her up the bank to the house, where the girls had already sped, calling for help.

The doctor had come in a few moments before and was sitting with his wife on the porch.

"Hark!" she exclaimed, "that is Marcia's voice. Oh, Charlie, what is it? What has happened? Something is wrong!"

She sprang up and ran swiftly through to the back of the house as she spoke, her husband following close behind her.

They met Ada and Marcia flying up the path from the back gate.

"Oh, father! Mother!" screamed the latter, "it's Fan. She's in the water! In the river! Percy has jumped in after her, and I'm afraid they'll both drown."

Before she had finished her sentence, her father had pushed past her and darted down the path to the riverbank.

When he reached it, the lads were halfway up with their unconscious burden. He paused and, as they drew near, took it from them.

"Percy?" he asked hoarsely.

"He's down there—on the pier—exhausted. He'll be all right directly," Stuart Ormsby answered with an effort. And waiting to hear no more, the doctor sped back to the house with little Fan in his arms.

He found Mildred there, calmly, swiftly preparing everything for him, Marcia and Ada assisting under her direction.

"Oh, that is right!" he said, "there is not a moment to be lost."

"Is she—?" Mildred began, but the appealing, anguished look in her eyes alone finished the question.

"I cannot tell, love," he answered in tremulous accents. "But we will use every effort to restore animation, and, please God, we will succeed, if it takes hours of exertion."

"She has not been long in the water?" he asked, his glance directing the question to his nephew.

"I—I don't know," stammered Stuart. "It seemed an age, but I hardly suppose it was really over five or ten minutes."

There was no sign of life then nor even after a half-hour's continuous and vigorous effort to restore warmth and respiration.

Then the mother's heart sank, the hot tears streamed over her cheeks.

"Mother's little Fan, mother's darling baby girl!" she moaned as she chafed the cold limbs and pressed her lips to them again and again.

"Do not despair, love," her husband said. "I do

not," he added, trying to speak cheerfully and even to smile, though it was but a poor attempt. So they worked and prayed on for another hour and at last were rewarded by the opening of the sweet eyes that had seemed to be closed forever and a faint whisper from the pale lips, "Mother, I'm so tired!"

Then, again, the mother's tears fell fast as she clasped her recovered darling to her heart. And even the father, strong, courageous man that he was, wept and sobbed aloud, but there was no bitterness in those tears—they were but the outpouring of a joy and gratitude that was beyond words.

The sisters and brothers, cousins, and other near and dear ones waiting, weeping, and praying in the next room, were soon told the glad tidings, and their anxiety and grief turned to joy and thankfulness unbounded.

It had been a time of agonizing suspense, especially to the brothers and sister. It would have been some slight relief to them, could they have busied themselves about the person of the little girl, joining in the efforts to restore animation, but there was room there for only the father and mother, who would by no means resign the work for a moment to any other hands. So the most Marcia and her brothers could do was to be ready for instant service, in hastening up and down, in and out, with anything the doctor called for.

It was past midnight when at last the announcement was made, "She is living. She breathes and she has spoken."

"Oh, praise the Lord!" exclaimed the grandfather. "Let us give thanks!" And, all falling on their knees, he led them in a fervent prayer, thanking God for the child's spared life and asking that she might be speedily and fully restored to her wonted health and strength.

Then, with an exchange of tearful, affectionate good nights, they withdrew to their homes, leaving Marcia and her brothers alone together, for the doctor, on communicating his joyful tidings, had gone back immediately to his charge.

Stuart hastened to the back part of the house to fasten the doors and windows for the night. Percy secured the front door after the departing friends, then turned to find Marcia leaning against the wall, pale, trembling, and looking ready to drop.

"Oh, Mar!" he said, catching her in his arms, "all this has been too much for you! Please don't cry, dear," he added, as she dropped her head on his shoulder and burst into tears and sobs. "It is over now and our darling little sister quite safe—I hope, I believe."

"O Percy! If she had never come to, how could we have borne it?"

"It would have been dreadful," he said tremulously, "particularly for me, because I persuaded mother to consent to her going.

"But I cannot think how it happened, how she came to be thrown out into the water. The jar of the boat striking against the pier was no heavier than it has been many a time without causing any such accident."

"I ought to have warned her that it was coming," said Marcia. "I remember now that she had been very quiet for some minutes. Percy, could she have fallen asleep, do you think?"

"I hadn't thought of that," he exclaimed, "but probably it is the true explanation. And I blame myself for inexcusable carelessness in failing to watch and warn her."

"I think that was more my proper task than yours," she said. "And, oh, I should never have forgiven myself if—if the darling had—had been drowned. I can hardly do so as it is."

"Well, don't trouble yourself with useless regrets," he said affectionately. "And do go directly to bed, for you look really ill."

"No, I want to take mother's place and let her rest and sleep."

"She won't let you."

"No, certainly not," said their father's voice close at hand. "Neither she nor I will leave Fan for some hours yet, and you three must go at once to your beds."

# CHAPTER XXI

AFTER SOME HOURS of refreshing sleep, Fan woke to find both parents beside her bed, both gazing at her with faces full of tender concern.

"Why," she said, "what's the matter? Have I been sick?"

"You are doing very well now, my pet," her father replied in tremulous tones. But Mildred only bent over her and kissed her tenderly several times.

"How happy you both look, father and mother, and yet your eyes are full of tears!" said the child wonderingly. "Oh, I remember! I fell into the river. Did you think I was drowned?"

"We feared so for a while," replied her father, leaning over her and smoothing her hair caressingly. "But God has been very good to you and to us. He has spared your life and saved us all from a sore bereavement, for our little Fan is very dear to father, mother, brothers, and sister."

An awed look came over her face, and she lay for a moment silently thinking. Then, lifting glad, tearful eyes, she said, "Yes, God was very good to keep me from drowning. I'm glad I'm alive this morning. I don't want to leave you yet, mother dear, nor father, either. Or Marcia or my brothers. No, nor any of the others—so many that I love and that love me.

"But it's daylight! The sun's shining! Have you been up all night with me? Oh, how tired you must be, mother! You, too, father. Can't you go and sleep some now?"

"Presently," replied her father. "Marcia is getting her breakfast now, then she will sit with you while your mother and I eat and sleep. I think we will be able to do both, now we know that our dear little girl is spared to us."

Even as the words left his lips, Marcia came in softly. Her eyes shone with pleasure at the sight of Fan looking very nearly herself again.

"Oh, Fan darling, how glad I am!" she exclaimed, hurrying to the bedside to embrace her little sister.

"You look pale and tired, Mar," Fan said, holding her fast and looking up lovingly into her face. "But not so tired and white as mother does."

"Mother will look better when she has had her breakfast," the doctor said, rising. "Come, my love, let us go down and eat. Marcia will take good care of our patient. I am not afraid to trust her," he added, smiling affectionately upon his eldest daughter.

"Nor I," said Mildred, giving Marcia her own seat by the bedside. "She could not be more trustworthy if she were as old as her mother."

They found Percy in the dining room moving restlessly about. He gave them an appealing look as they came in.

"How is she now, father?" he asked with emotion.

"Quite herself again," the doctor answered cheerfully.

"And you have not a word of reproach for me, father, mother?"

"No, no! We do not see that anyone was to blame," they both said. "It seems to have been an accident, though we do not understand exactly how it happened."

"Marcia thinks Fan may have fallen asleep, for she remembers that the child was very quiet for a few moments before the accident."

"Ah! That is probably the explanation," said his father. "But we will not question her about it for a day or two. I want her kept as quiet as may be at present."

They did not question her, and indeed discouraged the child from talking about the subject till she was entirely recovered and had introduced it herself.

Only her mother and Marcia were with her at the time. They were sewing, Fan sitting by with a book, but for the last few minutes it had lain idly in her lap while she sat with her eyes fixed meditatively upon the carpet.

"What is my little girl thinking of?" asked Mildred, observing the thoughtfulness of her countenance.

"About that row on the river, mother, and my fall into the water."

"Oh, Fan, were you asleep, dear?" asked Marcia.

"Yes, I must have been. But the jar—of the boat striking against the pier, wasn't it?—and the plunge backward into the cold water waked me.

"Oh, mother, I was so frightened! I went down to the bottom, then up again, and I tried to catch at something, but my hands didn't touch anything but the water. And the current was sweeping me along so fast! I thought I was lost, and I prayed to God to save me from drowning or take me to heaven.

"Then I felt myself sinking down, down again, and I didn't know anything more till I opened my eyes in my own bed and saw you and father leaning over me."

With the last words, she rose, ran to her mother, and threw her arms around her neck.

Dropping her work, Mildred drew the child into her lap and held her close.

"Mother," said Fan, "how was I taken out of the river? No one has told me yet."

"Percy, your brother, saved you, darling."

"Did he jump in after me?"

"Yes, dear."

"Then he risked his own life to save mine? Oh, I am thankful he wasn't drowned! Nor I either."

"I think no one can be more thankful than your mother is," Mildred said in low, tender tones.

"And now, my darling, what are you going to do with the life God has so kindly spared to you?"

"Devote it to His service, mother, if I can find out just what He wants me to do."

"First give yourself to Him, then study His word to learn His will, and, as you find out each duty, try to perform it.

"'Whatsoever he saith unto you, do it.' Look to Him for guidance, and He will lead you on step by step."

"Mother," said Marcia, looking up brightly, "it is such a comfort to me that it is only one step at a time, instead of having to be able to see the way all along, at the start, from beginning to end."

"And if we hold fast to Jesus, we're safe," added Fan. "Oh, I mean always to hold tight to him."

"I hope you will, dear," said Mildred, "but the safety is in being held fast by Him. He says of his sheep, 'I give unto them eternal life; and they shall never perish, neither shall any man pluck them out of my hand. My Father, which gave them me, is greater than all; and no man is able to pluck them out of my Father's hand. I and my Father are one.'

"Our weak wills are liable to change. Our sinful hearts and the temptations of Satan and the world might lead us to let go our hold upon Christ, but nothing can loosen His grasp upon us if once we are within His hand.

"'. . . for I am persuaded, that neither death, nor life, nor angels, nor principalities, nor powers, nor things present, nor things to come, nor height, nor depth, nor any other creature, shall be able to separate us from the love of God, which is in Christ Jesus our Lord.'"

"Oh, mother," said Marcia, "there is such comfort in those texts when one's heart trembles and is afraid in looking forward to all the troubles and trials that may come in the long, long journey of life—if we are to live to be old—or the passage through the dark valley of the shadow of death, which may be very near."

"Yes, daughter, in those and in many others.

"'As thy days, so shall thy strength be.'

"'Fear not, for I am with thee.'

"'I will never leave thee, nor forsake thee.'

"Yes, without the great and precious promises of God's word, I should greatly dread the future for myself and all my dear ones, not knowing what it may have in store for any of us. But, having them, we may go bravely forward, fearing nothing.

"'The Lord is my light and my salvation; whom shall I fear? The Lord is my strength of my life; of whom shall I be afraid?'"

"Mother," said Fan, "I remember that the Bible calls life a race to be run, and a battle to fight."

"Yes, a race that must be run, a battle that must be fought, by each one who would inherit eternal life. But it is not a race in which only one will receive the prize; it will be given to all who run aright.

"'So run that ye may obtain,' says the apostle."

"How, mother?"

"Diligently, earnestly, patiently, with care to keep in the right path—the strait and narrow way that leads to eternal life—looking continually to Jesus, treading in his footsteps, striving to copy his example in everything.

"Paul uses their races as an illustration. It was the custom in them to hang up a crown or garland at the goal, and the one who first reached and laid hold of it might take it down and have it as a reward.

"'And every man that striveth for the mastery is temperate in all things.' So must we be in running our race. 'Now they do it to obtain a corruptible crown; but we an incorruptible.'"

Marcia sighed. "Mother, it seems very hard and discouraging that one's whole life must be the running of a race and the fighting of a battle!"

"Ah! But think of the glorious prize to be won—the crown of righteousness which the Lord, the righteous Judge, shall give to all them who love his appearing! Think of the armor he has provided for the defense of his soldiers: the girdle of truth, 'having your loins girt about with truth'; the breastplate of righteousness (the imputed righteousness of Christ, which He is ready to bestow on all who earnestly seek it of Him); the shield of faith; the helmet of salvation; 'the sword of the spirit, which is the word of God.'

"Encased in that armor, daughter, and fighting under the Captain of our salvation, the Lord Jesus Christ, we need fear nothing; the victory is assured. We shall be 'more than conquerors, through Him that loved us.'

"It is true that 'we wrestle not against flesh and blood, but against principalities, against powers, against the rulers of the darkness of this world, against spiritual wickedness in high places:' but strong as they are, Jesus is still stronger. And if we put on the whole armor which he has provided and trust in him, we shall be—we are—safe.

"'They shall never perish, neither shall any pluck them out of my hand.'"

"Mother," questioned Fan, "what is meant by principalities and powers and spiritual wickedness in high places?"

"Satan and his hosts. Jesus represents him as a monarch, with other fallen angels subject to him. They are like him in character—full of hatred, envy, malice, and all wickedness—and are obedient to his wicked will. They are enemies to God and man, and they use their utmost endeavors to rob God of His glory and men of their souls. They are watchful to tempt us to wrongdoing, to suggest evil thoughts, to harass God's people with doubts and fears. If they cannot destroy, they will do all they can to trouble and torment."

"But Jesus is stronger than all of them put together," said Fan thoughtfully. "Oh, mother, I am so glad of that!"

"Yes, dear, and so am I. Otherwise, there would be no hope for us, sinful and weak creatures that we are! But Jesus is almighty, able to save to the uttermost all that come unto God by Him. He is our Rock, our Defense, our Fortress, and, hidden in Him, we are perfectly safe. But we must make very sure that we are on the Rock, in the Fortress, for only there are we safe. Outside, we have no defense from our strong, wily, spiritual foes."

"Mother," said Marcia, "how can anyone who reads the Bible deny the divinity of Christ? Surely he asserts it very distinctly when he says, 'I and my Father are one.' And again, 'Verily, verily, I say unto you, before Abraham was, I am.'"

"Yes," said her mother, "and, indeed, I do not see how the statement could be made more plainly and emphatically than it is, again and again, in the Scriptures.

"John, in the first chapter of his Gospel, tells us, 'In the beginning was the Word, and the Word was with God, and the Word was God. The same was in the beginning with God. All things were made by him; and without him was not anything made that was made.'"

"But, mother, how are we sure that the Word there means Jesus?" asked Fan.

"It is made very evident in the fourteenth verse," said Mildred. And opening the Bible, she read aloud.

"'And the Word was made flesh, and dwelt among us, (and we beheld his glory, the glory as of the only begotten of the Father,) full of grace and truth.'"

Then, turning to the ninth chapter of Isaiah, she read,

"'Unto us a child is born, unto us a son is given; and the government shall be upon his shoulders; and his name shall be called Wonderful, Counsellor, The mighty God, The everlasting Father, The Prince of peace.'

"These," she said, "are only a few of the multitude of passages that teach the divinity of Christ. The Bible is full of it, and it is a most important doctrine, for if He were not God but only a perfect, sinless man, He would not be able to save from sin and hell."

"And He is the only Saviour. If He cannot save us, we are lost, for 'neither is there salvation in any other: for there is none other name under heaven given among men whereby we must be saved.'"

"Mother," said Marcia, "I have heard people say, 'It doesn't matter what you believe, if you are only sincere.'"

"That is a very great mistake," replied Mildred. "It is entirely contrary to the teachings of Scripture, even those of the text I have just quoted. Jesus tells us: 'I am the Way,' and this text that He is the only way. He tells us, also, that he is the door, and says, 'Verily, verily, I say unto you, He that entereth not by the door into the sheepfold, but climbeth up some other way, the same is a thief and a robber.'

"The bible is God's word, given us to teach us what to believe as well as what to do. And if we neglect to study it, to learn what its teachings are, or if having studied it, we refuse to believe them, are we not to blame?

"'He that believeth not God, hath made him a liar.' Truth remains the same, whether we choose to accept or deny it. Suppose one swallows poison. Will either ignorance of its properties or a determined refusal to believe in its hurtfulness save him from the natural consequences of his act?"

"No, mother, of course not. And equally, of course, a belief in some other than God's appointed way of salvation will not prevent the loss of the soul. Oh, mother, how important it is that we should believe aright! And how thankful we should be for the Bible to teach us what is truth!"

"Yes, and how we ought to exert ourselves to send it to those who have it not!"

Percy and Stuart had come into the room a few moments before, and the former now joined in the conversation.

"In business matters, a man doesn't find that his belief makes any difference in the fact. He may make a speculation, believing as strongly as possible that it is an excellent one and will prove very remunerative, and yet it may turn out most disastrous, in which case he will lose just as heavily as if he had not had any expectation of success."

"Mother," said Fan, "in that text you quoted a while ago, where Paul speaks of the crown laid up for him, you remember he adds, 'and not to me only, but unto all them also that love his appearing.' What does he mean by that?"

"The second coming of Jesus Christ. You know it is spoken of in very many places in the Bible. Jesus told his disciples that he would come again and bade them watch and be ready.

"Also, the angels who appeared to them as they stood gazing up steadfastly toward heaven, while He ascended out of their sight, said to them:

"'Ye men of Galilee, why stand ye gazing up into heaven? This same Jesus, which is taken up from you into heaven, shall so come in like manner as ye have seen him go into heaven.'"

"How soon, mother?"

"That, my child, no one can tell. Jesus said:

"'But of that day and hour knoweth no man, no, not the angels of heaven, but my Father only.'

"He told his disciples, too, that His coming would be very unexpected—like that of a thief in the night. He said, 'Watch therefore; for ye know not what hour your Lord doth come.'

"'Therefore, be ye also ready: for in such an hour as ye think not the Son of man cometh.'

"Let us obey. Let us strive to keep our hearts so full of love to Him that, should He come at any day or hour, we may be ready to meet Him with joy unbounded, and that we will be ever looking forward with longing for His appearing, praying, as the apostle John does in the last chapter of the Bible, 'Even so, come Lord Jesus.'

"Surely, those to whom he is indeed the 'chiefest among ten thousand' and 'the one altogether lovely' must love his appearing and rejoice in the possibility that it may be near at hand."

Fan had taken up a Bible and was glancing over the last chapter of Revelation.

"Mother," she said, "I don't understand. Jesus says here, 'Surely, I come quickly. Amen.' Yet nearly two thousand years have passed, and He has not come yet."

"If you will turn to second Peter, third chapter

and eighth verse, I think you will find the answer to the question in your mind," said Mildred. "You may read the passage aloud."

Fan obeyed.

"'But, beloved, be not ignorant of this one thing, that one day is with the Lord as a thousand years, and a thousand years as once day.'"

"You may read on," her mother said, as she paused at the end of the verse.

"'The Lord is not slack concerning his promise, as some men count slackness, but is long-suffering to usward, not willing that any should perish, but that all should come to repentance. But the day of the Lord will come as a thief in the night; in the which the heavens shall pass away with a great noise, and the elements shall melt with fervent heat, the earth also, and the works that are therein shall be burned up.'

"'Seeing then that all these things shall be dissolved, what manner of persons ought ye to be in all holy conversation and godliness.'"

"'A thousand years as one day,'" repeated the little girl meditatively. "According to that way of counting, it isn't two days yet since Jesus said he wold come again quickly. Mother, how soon will he come, do you suppose?"

"My dear child, I do not know at all. It is God's will that neither men nor angels shall know the day or hour, but He would have us live in a state of constant readiness for His coming. Many times Jesus repeated His warning to His disciples to watch and be ready, for His coming would be as that of a thief in the night and would find the world at large as unprepared for it as it was for the flood in the days of Noah.

"We are to watch constantly, diligently, yet patiently.

"'The Lord direct your hearts into the love of God, and the patient waiting for Christ.' 'He that believeth shall not make haste.'

"It is unbelief that makes us impatient of delay in any of God's providences."

# Chapter XXII

"Percy," said Fan, going to her brother, putting her arms round his neck, and kissing him, with tears in her eyes, "thank you for saving my life. Oh, it was ever so good of you to jump into the river after me!"

"Not at all, little sister," he replied as he drew her to a seat upon his knee. "I hardly deserve thanks for rescuing you from danger you had been brought into by my carelessness."

"It wasn't your fault that I went to sleep," she returned.

"So you were asleep?"

"Yes, and if I had kept awake like a good girl," she said with a little laugh, "I'd have held fast, of course, and not have been thrown into the water. So I was the only one to blame."

"Ah, but it was my doing that you went."

"Yes, you wanted to give me pleasure and didn't think there was any danger. And there wouldn't have been if I had kept awake. So there, now! You are not to blame yourself anymore," she added, repeating her hug and kiss.

"That's very generous of you, little sister," Percy said, returning her caresses. "It has been a mystery to us all how the accident happened—though Mar suggested that probably you had fallen asleep—but now it is clear enough. Another time we will watch over you carefully and make sure that you are awake, or somebody is holding on to you, when we are nearing the pier."

Fan—as the youngest and a very lovable child—had always been much humored and indulged by her relatives, especially her brothers, sisters, and cousin Stuart. It had not seemed to injure her heretofore, but after her narrow escape from sudden death, there was such an increase of the familial affection, particularly on the part of the boys, that her mother began to fear she would be quite spoiled.

But her father—as much inclined as anybody else to indulge the little maid—said, "Never fear, Milly, my love; it is good for the boys and won't hurt the child in the least."

Nor did it. It only made her happier than ever, though a joyous, merry little maiden she had always been, loved by everybody who knew her, and loving them all in return.

Busy as the lads were with their studies, they found time for a number of long talks with Mildred. Percy was of the opinion that he could hardly find a better or wiser counsellor than his mother, and Stuart very nearly agreed with him. Aunt Mildred, he thought, was almost as sensible and well-informed as his own father and mother, perhaps quite as much so as the latter, who was less interested than her sister in some of the topics he and Percy wished to discuss.

It was a dear delight to the young people of both families to gather about her for a chat, when she was at leisure to listen and reply, which was generally in the cool of the evening, when the day's work was done, and she and they would sit on the porch enjoying a well-earned rest.

On one of these occasions, Percy opened the conversation with a question: "Mother, would you like your sons to be politicians?"

"Yes, but not partisans," she said. "I hope they will always put the best interests of their country far before those of any political party and set their faces steadfastly against any mean, underhand, unlawful effort to advance party interests.

"I trust you will never engage in, or even wink at, any proceeding that will not bear the full light of day, and never help to put a bad man into any office, great or small.

"If the choice must be between a corrupt man of your own party and an honest, upright one belonging to the other, by all means vote for the latter.

"The Bible says, 'As a roaring lion, and a ranging bear, so is a wicked ruler over the poor people.'"

"I am afraid," remarked Stuart Ormsby, "that the choice is oftener between two not particularly upright men, the business of nominating being generally left to the back-room politicians."

"And why is it left to them?" returned Mildred with some indignation in her tones.

"Well, auntie," said Stuart, "I often hear gentlemen say they don't care to vote and won't have anything to do with politics because it has become such a dirty business (morally, of course, they mean), being so entirely in the hands of the baser sort of fellows—the drinking, carousing sort, who care nothing for the good of the country, or right or justice, but engage in politics as a business, to fill their own pockets at the public expense."

"If it is a dirty business now," said Mildred, "the right kind of men should take hold of it and make it a clean one. Doubtless the task would be a difficult one, but what ought to be done can be done, if those whose duty it is will only set about it with sufficient energy and determination, with patriotism enough to be willing to make sacrifices of time and labor for the good of the land of their birth.

"My boys have fought for their country," she went on, regarding them with a proud smile, "and I hope they will one day show that they love her well enough to work for her also, even though the work be both distasteful and laborious."

"Then you want us to be politicians?" queried Percy.

"Yes, in the proper sense of the word: 'one versed in the science of government.' We need pure politicians, men who will do all in their power to promote the best interests of the country, remembering that 'righteousness exalteth a nation: but sin is a reproach to any people.'

"Oh, my heart's desire and prayer to God for my country is, 'May we be that nation whose God is the Lord'!"

"If the mothers were all like you, Aunt Mildred," Stuart said, "I think we would be such a nation."

"A great deal depends upon the mothers," she returned. "The wives, sisters, and daughters also have a great deal of influence, and by exerting it on the right side may do much for their country."

"I'm glad we can help a little in some way," said Marcia.

"Yes," said their aunt Annis, who, though one of the group, had not joined in the conversation thus far, "and I sometimes think that the good, sensible, intelligent, honest men who ought to rule this country are not treating us women right in neglecting that duty. They deny us any share in the making and executing of the laws, or in choosing those who should do that work, and then refuse to attend to it properly themselves.

"I, for one, am entirely willing that the land should be ruled by American men of the right sort, but I do feel indignant when they allow the power to get into the hands of bad, unscrupulous men, often foreigners who neither know nor care anything about our institutions."

"It is too bad, auntie," Percy said. "I should be indignant, too, if I were a woman. Indeed, I believe I am, as a boy, not yet entitled to a vote. I see no justice in giving that privilege to men who haven't been in the country long enough to know anything about our institutions, and denying it to lads of my age, native-born citizens who have studied the subject till they understand it better than many of those fellows ever will."

"Never mind, Percy. You and I will have our turn three years hence," said his cousin in a tone of satisfaction.

"Yes, and use it aright, I trust," responded Percy.

"Aunt Annis, are you a woman's rights woman?" asked Marcia.

"If you mean by that, Do I want to vote? I answer no," replied Annis emphatically. "I should far rather leave politics to the men—my countrymen who are honest and patriotic, understand our institutions, and desire to perpetuate them—if they will only attend faithfully to the business."

"We women must make it our care to stir them

241

up to it," said Mildred, "each one endeavoring to influence her own male relatives and friends."

"Well," laughed Annis, "there doesn't seem to be much for me to do in that way. My brothers are all older than I, all away from home except Rupert. And he, I am sure, needs no stirring up on the matter. I have no other near male relatives except these lads to whom you are attending yourself, Milly."

"But you may, and probably will, have opportunities to exert your influence with your gentlemen friends and sometimes those whom you meet casually," Mildred returned lightly.

"I am pretty sure that if you keep on the lookout for opportunities, you will find them. Besides, you may be, someday, a wife and mother like your older sisters."

"Mother," Marcia said as they sat together at their sewing the next day, "I want to lead a useful life, but a woman doesn't seem to have as great opportunities for usefulness as a man."

"Doesn't she? How do you suppose the men would get along without us? I have a notion they would find it but a sorry sort of world," returned Mildred with an amused yet tender smile into her daughter's serious, half-troubled face. "Ask your father what he thinks about it."

"Oh, I know well enough that father would say he could never live without you and that you are quite as useful as he is, if not more so. And I don't know how we children could do without either you or him."

"Then you think, after all, that women may be as useful as men if they are wives and mothers?"

"Yes, ma'am, but all women don't marry."

"No, and I should be sorry to have my daughters

feel that marriage is absolutely necessary to either happiness or usefulness, so far as they themselves are concerned."

"I should be very sorry, too, mother, if I felt so, because I don't want ever to leave you and father."

Mildred smiled slightly at that. "No, dear child," she said in tender tones, "and it would be a hard trial to us to be called upon to give you up to someone else. When the thought of such a possibility intrudes into my mind, I try to banish it and be happy in the present."

"I don't think you need fear it at all, mother dear," said Marcia. "And as I am not likely to marry, I want to learn how I can be most useful as a single woman at home with her father and mother."

"You are very useful now, daughter," returned the mother, smiling affectionately upon the fair girl, "a great help and comfort to father, mother, brothers, and sister. I consider you an accomplished needlewoman and a thorough housekeeper. If I should be laid aside by illness, I could trust all household cares to you without the least anxiety that anything should be neglected or done amiss. And if I were called away to the better land, you would be fully capable of attending to your father's comfort and would not neglect it, I know."

"Oh, mother, don't speak of that!" cried Marcia with tears in her eyes.

"It will not come any the sooner for speaking of it, dearest," Mildred said gently, "and neither you nor I can tell which will be taken first. But we may comfort ourselves with the thought that when we are called to part, it will be for only a time, and when we meet again, it will be to part no more forever.

"But, to go back to the subject we began with, I think that even a man could not have higher work than that of a wife and mother—the training of her children for usefulness here and glory hereafter, making home happy and comfortable for them and her husband, and helping him with his cares and burdens by her sympathy and perhaps advice, if she be a wise enough woman to give good advice and he a man wise enough to afford her the opportunity.

"And for single women there are many walks of usefulness. There is much to be done in the church, and in the world, that they can do quite as well as the men, or better.

"Then a woman, as well as a man, may earn money and do good with it, though I must acknowledge that the earning is not often so easy to her as to him, women being usually paid much less for doing the same work and doing it quite as well or even better."

"Yes, mother, I know that," said Marcia, "and it does seem unjust, especially as women are weaker than men. But don't you think girls should be trained to some business, as boys are, so that they will know what to do for a living if they ever need to earn one for themselves?"

"Yes," Mildred said, "your father and I both think it will be the kindest thing we can do for you and Fan, for, though he is now able to provide for you, the money may be lost by him, or by you after it comes into your possession, for there is no possibility of so securing earthly riches that they may not take wings and fly away.

"And besides, should you live single, you will be all the happier for having an occupation, for having an object in life.

"Therefore, we have been very glad to find that you have a decided talent for drawing. We intend to give you every opportunity to cultivate it, hoping that you may be able to become a designer and, as such, capable of making a good living for yourself."

"Designing what, mother?" the young girl asked with a bright, pleased look.

"Whatever you find you have taste and talent for. It may be patterns for carpets, calicoes, muslins, or other fabrics, or perhaps designs for engravers of illustrations for books and periodicals."

"Oh, mother! It would be work I should delight in!" cried Marcia, her face sparkling with pleasure. "And I should like it all the better because I could do it at home, and if I don't need to earn money for my own support, it would be very nice to make some to do good with."

"Very nice, indeed!" returned her mother. "And now, I hope, you are quite reconciled to being only a girl, with the prospect of never being anything more than a woman," she added laughingly.

"Oh, mother! I never wanted to be anything else! I wouldn't, on any account, be turned into a boy if I could," responded Macia, blushing vividly.

"No, I am quite sure of that, dear. I was only jesting with you," Mildred answered soothingly.

"I think I should like to do that, too, and I mean to take the greatest pains with my drawing lessons," spoke up Fan, who had been sitting by, a silent listener to the conversation, her fingers meanwhile busily fashioning a bonnet for her doll. "Do you think I could do it, mother? I mean, do you think I might learn to be a designer?"

"I have little doubt of it, provided you diligently

cultivate your talent," Mildred answered, "for you, too, show a decided talent for drawing, though hardly so great as your sister's."

"Look, mother, it's done, and isn't it pretty?" cried the little girl, holding up the now completed doll's bonnet.

"Yes, dear, very pretty," replied Mildred. "It shows that you have both taste and skill in that direction."

"Yes, mother, I hope so, and I do enjoy making bonnets—and dresses, too—for my doll. I believe I'd like to be a milliner and dressmaker, but Ada says it wouldn't be genteel to have a trade and work at it."

"I am sorry to hear that Ada feels and talks in that way," Mildred remarked with gravity. "There is nothing degrading in following any honest and useful occupation. The Apostle Paul worked at tentmaking, and it is said the Master himself was a carpenter, working at that trade with His reputed father, Joseph."

"Yes, mother, and I don't see any reason why dressmaking and millinery should be thought less genteel than carpenter work or tent making. And I know you have always taught us idleness is a sin, because God's command is, 'six days shalt thou labour, and do all thy work.'"

"Yes," said Marcia, "and the Bible bids us, 'Study to be quiet, and to do your own business, and to work with your own hands, as we commanded you; that you may walk honestly toward them that are without, and that ye may have lack of nothing.' It says, too, that 'an idle soul shall suffer hunger.' Also, 'He becometh poor that dealeth with a slack hand: but the hand of the diligent maketh rich.' And, 'This we commanded you, that if any would not work, neither should he eat.'"

"You see," said their mother, "that there is no foundation in Scripture for the idea that there is any degradation in honest labor but that, on the contrary, it is altogether opposed to the teachings of God's work. Therefore, those who profess to be His children should not give it any countenance, and if anyone despise and scorn us because we obey His command, 'work with your own hands,' let us remember that we are told, 'the friendship of the world is enmity with God.' And oh, how much better to live in the light of His countenance than to be admired, courted, and flattered by all the world!"

# CONCLUSION

THE DAY THAT saw the lads on their way to college was a sad one to the mothers and sisters (fathers and brother seemed to feel it less) yet joyful in comparison to that other day of parting, when they were setting out on their way to the battlefield with the dreadful possibility of becoming food for powder, shot, or shell staring them in the face.

But Mildred felt it sorely as the beginning of the breaking up of the family life that had been so sweet. Her boy would come back a man and perhaps would soon be setting up a home for himself. The young man would doubtless be her pride and delight, but the boy whose place he would take had been very dear, and she could not banish a heartache at the thought that he was gone to return no more.

However, she did not give way to her depression but struggled determinately against it and presently conquered it in a measure, then set herself to work to cheer and comfort her weeping daughters, who thought that mother's face and manner could hardly be so bright and cheery if her heart were quite so sad as theirs over Percy's going.

"Oh, mother," sobbed Marcia, "it seems as if half the house is gone!"

"Yes, dear, but that won't last. We will grow accustomed to our dear boy's absence as we do to other trying things. By a wise and merciful ordering of Providence, we are enabled to grow in a manner so used to things that are at first unpleasant, or even painful, that at length we can endure them quite easily."

"Yes, mother," responded Fan, "even when it is bad, bitter medicine. You know father gave me a tonic once when I was weak, and at first I could hardly bear to take it, it was so bad, so bitter. But after a while, I almost liked the taste."

"It is so with very many things," Mildred said. "I have often thought life would be almost unendurable after the death of any very near and dear one, if sorrow were to keep its keen edge always. But time, mercifully, dulls it, and we partially forget our grief in the occupations and interests of our daily life.

"So it will be, dears, with this sorrow of separation. Besides, let us remember that it is not unmixed evil. We want Percy to gain a finished college education, and he will write to us, and his letters will be a source of great enjoyment. It will be pleasant to write to him, too. And both these pleasures will grow out of this separation from him that now seems so painful."

"Mother, you are the best kind of a comforter!" exclaimed Marcia. "Yes, it will be quite delightful to correspond with him. And then his letters can be treasured up and enjoyed over again years hence."

"Besides," Mildred went on, "there is the pleasure of looking forward to his coming home again, and I trust the hope of showing him great improvement when he comes will stimulate his sisters to great diligence in their studies and everything in which there is room for improvement."

"Oh, yes, mother," they said, "in music and drawing especially, for Percy cares a great deal to see us improve in them."

"And the letter-writing will be improving, to us," added Marcia.

"It ought to be, and will be if you take pains with your style," Mildred replied.

And just there the talk was interrupted by the entrance of Dr. Landreth and Colonel Keith.

"What? Crying, girls?" exclaimed the latter in a bantering tone. "Now, if I were the sister of such a fine young fellow as Percy Landreth, I should be too proud and happy to think of shedding tears."

"Why, uncle, if he wasn't so nice — so good and kind and brave and everything that makes us fond and proud of him — we wouldn't be crying," said Fan with a sob, wiping her tearful eyes with her handkerchief.

At that, uncle Rupert burst into quite a eulogy on Percy, giving Stuart Ormsby a share in it also, telling of their brave deeds in the war that was now happily over and their unselfish kindness to friend and foe.

"Confederate prisoners sometimes met with unkind treatment, which made my blood boil with indignation when I saw it," he said in the course of his remarks. "But only from the cowards who kept in the rear, out of danger, never from the brave fighting men, for only cowards are cruel. But among such immense numbers as were gathered together in the Union armies, there will always be found some very wicked, unscrupulous men ready to take advantage of every opportunity to enrich themselves at the expense of anybody else and to indulge their love of cruelty in torturing any helpless thing that comes their way. They are a shame and disgrace to their fellows, an injury to any cause they may profess to espouse."

"Very true," said the doctor, "and their evil deeds have done, and I fear will do, much to delay or prevent the beginning and growth of kind, brotherly feeling between the late Confederates and those who stood by the Union.

"But it is sure to come finally, nevertheless. We are one people, bound together by many close, strong ties. To them, equally with ourselves, belongs the glorious heritage of this beautiful land. They are as truly a part of this great, powerful nation as we, and the time will come when they and we will rejoice together in its preservation as an undivided whole and will think the war — terrible and costly as it was — worth all it cost."

"Father," said Fan, "didn't the 'boys in blue' do as much for us as the soldiers of the Revolution?"

"And oughtn't they to be kept in remembrance with the same love and gratitude?" asked Marcia.

"Certainly," he said. "The soldiers of the Revolution suffered, fought, and bled that this great, free, glorious nation might have a beginning; the Union soldiers of the Civil War, that it might be perpetuated to us and to our children with all its blessings.

"Those opposed to them fought bravely. We have reason to be proud of their courage, also, and their endurance, and many of them thought they were fighting for their country. Their education was in fault. They had been taught the heresy of 'states' rights' and did not see the danger of it —

how, if carried out, it would lead to universal anarchy. Their hearts were right; but their heads were so wrong that those who would preserve the Union were compelled to resist them as we would an insane though good man who, in his irresponsible frenzy, was mistakenly trying to kill us and himself.

"It was a suicidal attempt on their part, though they knew it not. Like Paul, when he persecuted the Church, they did it ignorantly, in unbelief.

"But the time will come when they will rejoice as we do in their failure and the consequent preservation of the Union."

• • •

Twenty years have passed, and the doctor's prophecy seems to have found its fulfillment in the great and increasing material prosperity of the South and her love for the Union and the old flag, in both of which the whole nation rejoices. We are now indeed one people—one in interest, one in affection, one in patriotic love for our common country.

## THE END

# *The Original Elsie Classics*